DELIVERER

TAMARA HART HEINER

Deliverer
copyright 2013 Tamara Hart Heiner
cover art by Steven Novak

Also by Tamara Hart Heiner:
Perilous (WiDo Publishing 2010)
Altercation (WiDo Publishing 2012)
Priceless (WiDo Publishing 2016)

Inevitable (Tamark Books 2013)
Entranced (Tamark Books 2017)

Lay Me Down (Tamark Books 2016)
Reaching Kylee (Tamark Books 2016)

The Extraordinarily Ordinary Life of Cassandra Jones:
Walker Wildcats Year 1 (Tamark Books 2016)
Walker Wildcats Year 2 (Tamark Books 2016)

Tornado Warning (Dancing Lemur Press 2014)

CHAPTER 1

"There." Jeff Truman nodded his head toward the private car that had just pulled up to the posh hotel across the street. A balding, sunburned man climbed out, pushing a pair of sunglasses up his nose. A gold chain glinted around his neck. Several body guards flanked him.

Claber lifted his camera and snapped a picture. "McAllister."

"Maverick will be here soon." Truman pulled on his fingers, relishing the sound that released tension with each crack. "You sure this is a good idea?"

Claber's green eyes darted toward Truman before focusing on the beachfront hotel. "You mean, using them as bait to lure out the *Carnicero*?"

Bait. Truman gnawed his lower lip. Such a strong word. "They're not bait." Maybe they were. "If something goes wrong..." He let the sentence draw off.

"You're doing a service. It benefits all of us if we can learn the *Carnicero*'s identity. You're just the first person brave enough to risk catching him."

Claber said the words with such conviction that Truman almost believed him. It was, essentially, the truth. Every crime lord on the planet tiptoed around for fear of the unknown vigilante discovering them and destroying them.

And if Truman could provide that identity, his comrades might finally respect him. All it had taken was letting a few more details than necessary slip out to his associates as he discussed his upcoming meeting in Cancun. None of them would mean to betray him, but they would talk amongst themselves and to other people. With any luck, the *Carnicero* had ears to the ground.

"Maverick," Claber said as a bearded redhead exited a cab. He did a quick scan of the area before entering the hotel.

Truman glanced at Claber, poised with his digital camera as he watched the traffic. "I better get inside before they wonder where I am."

Claber frowned. "Wait. Where's Cisnero?"

"Her flight was delayed. She'll be here later. In the meantime, you take pictures of anyone going in or out of the hotel."

"And what if it is the *Carnicero*?" Claber said. "I won't know him. You won't know him until he comes in, guns blazing."

That was the problem with not knowing what a guy looked like. Perhaps including himself as bait hadn't been the best idea. "Trust your gut. If you think someone looks suspicious, send me a message. I'll get us out."

"Will do."

———

"You in or not, Truman?" Maverick, a large redhead who chewed his tobacco like an overgrown cow, smashed himself in front of Truman. His mouth smacked noisily and he gave a wide smile. "How about it? Can we convince you?"

Truman stared back at Maverick, taking in the glazed eyes and bovine expression. He half expected the idiot to moo. He lifted his gaze to peer out the windows behind Maverick. Sunshine reflected off the white sands of the Cancun beach, aqua waves rising and falling as if the ocean were sighing. For a moment, Truman imagined he wasn't here to meet with criminals and thug lords. Instead he was on a leisure trip with his dog Barley, a big golden lab who would enjoy a change of scenery from the Canadian forest.

Maverick snapped his fingers, the amused look gone from his face. He settled back in a cushioned chair around the conference table. "You in or not, Truman?"

They had tried this before. Multiple times, in fact.

Truman checked his phone, worried he'd miss a warning from Claber. Nothing so far. He leaned forward, closing his fingers together and resting them on the glass tabletop. "Truth is, gentleman, I'm quite content with my life as it is. Smuggling jewels may not bring me as much money as weapons, but it's not as dangerous, either. And I have enough to live off."

And then some. Truman had estates and residences all over the world. He paid his men generously. And of course he had a stash of money to buy off any suspicious authorities.

McAllister sneered, the salt-and-pepper stubble on his chin gave away his age. His lip curved up to expose glinting white teeth.

Here it comes, Truman thought.

"That's only because Daddy left you a nice kitty when he died, huh, Truman? How long you gonna play before it runs out? Time's coming when you can't hide in your castle doing nothing."

"Maybe I'll retire when that happens," Truman replied with a shrug. His collar clung to his neck in the humid air. Might be hard to live the life of a law-abiding citizen. Then again, he had always tried to bend the rules rather than break them.

A noble boy. Who would not do thee right?

The line from Shakespeare's *King John* imprinted on his thoughts. Truman reflected on the meaning behind them. As long as he was the noble and good one, he was set.

McAllister growled, blue eyes narrowing over the red nose that matched the red skin of his bare head. "I know you think you're

3

better than us. That somehow you haven't dirtied your hands because all you do is steal. Well, that don't matter to some. You've got as much on you as the rest of us, and you're marked."

Interesting. It was as though McAllister had heard his thoughts. Truman kept his face passive and templed his fingers. "What do you mean?"

Maverick jumped in, pausing only to spit his wad of tobacco at the nearby trashcan. "The *Carnicero*. That's what he means."

McAllister glared at Maverick, but Truman had suspected that answer. "What about him?" Truman's question came out sharper than he intended. A trickle of fear tickled the palm of his hand, and he clenched his fist. He had to remind himself that speaking about the man wouldn't make him suddenly appear.

"We took great risk in arranging this meeting," McAllister hissed. He glanced at his five men who guarded the doors to the conference room.

"The *Carnicero* is tracking us," Maverick said, nodding his bushy redhead in emphasis. "We don't know how, but every time we meet, he seems to come along."

"He's always tracking us." Truman stood, grabbing his baseball cap and pulling it down low over his eyes. He kept his chin up and his lips straight, trying to mask his unease. "Let's wrap this up. It's a beautiful day out there, and the beach looks wonderful. We should all be enjoying it." If the *Carnicero* hadn't shown by now, he wasn't coming. Truman didn't know whether to feel relieved or disappointed.

McAllister's jaw worked for a moment before he got his words out. "He won't skip you, you know. You might not do the work your father did, but you're no golden boy."

"We can help." Like an excited puppy, Maverick was there again, eyes lighting up. "If you make one shipment of weapons, we'll get you stocked with a few big pieces. Set up an international safety net for you."

For a nanosecond, the offer tempted him. "Thanks, but my answer's still no. I'm safe where I am." Truman straightened. "I have a strong network already."

Truman turned his back and walked out of the conference room. Nobody called after him or tried to stop him. Probably they had known it was a waste of time before they even started.

———

Claber hadn't budged from his perch on the low wall across the street.

"Nothing?" Truman asked, as relieved as he was disappointed.

Claber shook his head. "I'll show you all the shots I got. But I didn't see anyone who struck me as suspicious."

"No, he didn't come. We would all be dead if he had." It had been a foolish endeavor. What had Truman thought, that the *Carnicero* would skip him over? McAllister was right. He might not deal in weapons or drugs, but he was no saint.

Truman narrowed his eyes at his second-in-command. Sunlight bounced off the buzzed-cut head. "Put some sunscreen on your head before you burn as bad as McAllister."

That brought a grim smile from his tall, muscular cohort. Claber snapped a few pictures of the scantily clad women on the busy street and put the camera away. "What time do we meet our man?" He scanned the crowd around them.

"He's not coming here." A taxi waited at the curb, and Truman stepped forward to snag it. "We'll take a taxi to his hotel after we stop by our room and get the cargo."

"His hotel?" Claber echoed. "Since when does Raminaji stay in a hotel?"

"Raminaji's dead. This is his successor, and he's understandably nervous."

Neither spoke during the twenty-minute drive to their hotel. They went up to their room, where Truman proceeded to take apart their suitcases, opening hidden pockets and unscrewing the handles.

"What about the carry-ons?" Claber asked. Those were trickier to hide jewels in, since they went through the cameras.

"Sewn into the bottom inside seams," Truman answered. "Loosen them, but don't remove the threads."

Claber plucked at a stitch with his fingernail. "This Grey's work?"

Truman piled a collection of gold necklaces, rubies, diamond earrings, and pearls onto the bed. "Man's a miracle with a needle."

"And in the kitchen." Claber's stomach growled.

Truman grunted his agreement and began adding up the retail value of the jewelry. His men were trained to grab a quick handful and leave the scene of a robbery as quickly as possible. They might not get the most expensive items, but they wouldn't get caught, either.

He had seven diamond wedding rings, two diamond solitaires, one $37,000 diamond and gold ring, and enough bracelets and necklaces to total almost $140,000.

Truman couldn't expect to get that, but he would get at least half. Sure, he could do better with drugs or weapons. But $70,000 once or twice a month more than covered his expenses.

"We won't be coming back to the hotel." Truman zipped up his bag. "Leave anything you don't need. I don't want the staff to know we're gone."

The taxi trip across town took nearly half an hour. Truman drummed his fingers on the armrest, one hand clutching the door handle. He wouldn't call himself nervous, but he'd lured the *Carnicero* here and had to be ready to get out at a moment's notice.

He wasn't well known down here. If they were stopped by Mexican authorities or the drug cartel, he could slip away with the jewels, unseen. Claber should be safe, as he had no contraband on him.

Truman's mind skipped back to Maverick's offer to join the weapon's trade. He received such offers frequently. To join the weapon's trade, the drug trade, the sex trade. He could make a lot more money.

But McAllister was right: Truman had money. His father had made sure of that.

The taxi arrived at a small, single-level hotel. Truman's eyes raked over the metal roofing and crumbling stucco.

"They don't show this one to the tourists," Claber murmured, sliding his head closer to Truman's.

They got out of the cab, and Truman pressed less than half the fare into the cabdriver's hand. The man opened his mouth to protest, but Truman stopped him. "Wait. Wait." He pointed toward the trunk where their luggage sat. "I pay you four times as much." He opened his hand to reveal much more than the required money.

The driver's eyes widened. He nodded quickly.

Taxi secured, Truman stopped in front of number 5 and knocked on the door. Claber puffed out his chest and fingered the inside of his jacket. Truman kept his gaze on the hotel.

The door cracked open. A heavy chain prevented the full extension, and thick smoke wafted out the crack.

"*Quién és? Quién és?*"

"*El Mano*." Truman hoped they wouldn't have to conduct this transaction in Spanish. "*Hablás inglés?*"

"*Sí, sí. Entren.* Come in."

His Mexican accent muffled the words so badly that at first Truman didn't realize he'd switched languages. But the door widened, and Claber went in first, flicking on lights and surveying the room even as Truman followed.

"What do we call you?" Truman asked the short, beady-eyed man in front of him.

"Fernando," the man said. His bloodshot eyes tracked Claber as Claber moved around the small bed and stepped into the bathroom. Sweat gathered on his upper lip.

"Relax, Fernando," Truman said. "He's securing the room."

Claber stepped out of the bathroom. "It's clean."

Fernando let out a soft breath. Judging from the fidget of his hands and the look in his eyes, Truman guessed there were drugs in here somewhere.

Claber gave the all clear and moved to the window to stand guard, adjusting the curtain to hide his face while peering out over the parking lot.

Truman reached into his jacket and removed the small satchel of jewels. "I'll display each item one at a time. You tell me what interests you and we negotiate."

Fernando's hand twitched. "I can't see all at once?"

"No." Truman shook his head. "We deal with one piece and then we move to the next." He knew from experience that showing all his jewels at once instantly gave the other person the upper hand. They would pay more for the pieces they really wanted and offer token prices for the others. Some had even tried to steal the jewels and run. Unbelievable that they would expect Truman to come in unarmed.

"How I pay?" Fernando scratched his eyebrow.

You are so stoned, my friend, Truman thought, *I could rob you and you wouldn't even know it.* "Cash. Up front."

"American dollars?"

"Mexican is fine."

Fernando's fingers twitched. "Okay."

One by one Truman lifted out each item, and they debated the price. Fernando was new at this. He offered money too low, and the bargaining took longer than usual.

Finally they reached an agreement. Fernando counted out the bills and Truman accepted them. "Next time, we do this faster. It shouldn't take this long."

"Sorry, sorry," Fernando mumbled.

"Let's go." Claber pulled the door open and they slipped out.

They kept to the shadows until away from the hotel, and then Truman hailed a cab. "*El banco, por favor*," Truman said. It didn't matter which bank. Any of them could do the transfer for him.

CHAPTER 2

"Thank you for visiting Mexico, Mr. Scotch," the Mexican airport official said, handing Truman back his Canadian passport.

Truman gave a brief nod. Claber followed, patting his fake passport in the palm of his hand.

Neither of them spoke as they finished up at the security checkpoint. They sat at their gate and waited for the airplane to arrive. Only when they were on board and taxiing down the runway did Truman exhale, letting his shoulders slump. He could relax now. They were on their way home.

Claber's phone vibrated in his pocket.

"You didn't turn your phone off," Truman chastized.

"I never do." Claber removed it from his pocket and thumbed over the message. "From Maverick." He glanced at Truman. "They were attacked."

Truman's shoulders tightened up again. "Where?"

Claber texted back and then scrolled through the response. "All of our hotels."

"Any fatalities?" Truman tightened his grip around the armrest.

"He doesn't say anything about McAllister. Maverick missed being there by a few hours, but he left two men behind to meet with Cisnero."

"And?" Truman knew the outcome without asking.

"Dead. Cisnero and Maverick's men."

Truman pushed back into the headrest, his heart thumping like a barrel drum in his chest. "What about McAllister?"

Claber's thumbs worked out the question. "Several of his men died, but he escaped."

"The *Carnicero*?"

"There's no proof."

"Of course." Truman nodded. "But who else could it be?"

Claber's phone vibrated as another text came through. "Here's a warning from Maverick. McAllister blames you. Thinks you knew."

"Was I so transparent?" Truman murmured.

"It's a lucky guess."

Claber squinted. "If it really was him, we just missed our chance. We have to get the upper hand, and fast."

Truman glanced toward the pocket where he knew Claber kept the camera. "Is it possible you got a picture?"

"I might. Maybe he's one of the guys I shot loitering around the hotel."

"Get prints made of every person you photographed. Let's see if we can't ID some faces."

The flight stalled in Dallas, and once again Truman told himself to avoid the DFW airport at all cost. The several hours' delay turned their flight into a red-eye. Truman tried to sleep, but he felt instant relief when the plane landed in Montreal.

The blond agent behind the customs desk had just stamped his passport when the phone began to ring. A quick glance at the display showed Sanchez's name. Truman's eyes flicked up to a digital clock above the baggage claim. Almost eight in the morning. Sanchez should be in Seattle, doing a quickie. Truman leaned against a square column and answered the phone. "Hello?"

"Boss." Sanchez's whisper struggled to get through the speaker. "Got a problem."

"Solve it," Truman snapped, not in the mood to baby him.

Sanchez continued as if he hadn't heard, which irritated Truman. If the men didn't get out soon, they'd risk getting caught. "We got half a million of jewels in the van."

"Then get out of there!" Truman hissed. He ran a hand through his short brown hair and looked around. No one watched him, except Claber.

"We can't," Sanchez whispered. "We're being held up. They've posted guards outside the exits, and someone's trying to steal our van."

It took a moment to analyze those words. Someone was holding his men up, while someone else tried to steal his van?

"What's wrong?" Claber mouthed.

Truman shook his head and said to Sanchez, "Do they have a car?"

"Yes, Boss. Parked in front of our van."

"They have weapons on you?"

"Big ones. Enough to take out the store."

Truman shoved a hand through his hair. They were in trouble.

The phone was plucked from Truman's hand, and he turned in surprise to see Claber speaking into it. "Take the rear exit," he instructed. "Kill the guards, and do it fast, before they realize what's happening. Take their car, dump the bodies, and get out of there."

"What are you doing?" Truman sputtered.

"Just do it!" Claber snarled into the phone. "It's you or them!" He jammed his finger onto the end button.

"Claber!" Truman hissed. He fisted his hands to hide his fury. Spots danced in front of his vision. "What are you doing?"

"I'm sorry, Boss." Claber lowered his eyes. "I know you don't like messes. But it was them or us."

"We could have just let them steal the van. I can afford a new

12

one. Now you've put Sanchez's entire team at risk."

"Word would get out," Claber countered. "Everyone would know you'd rather dump cargo than face a fight. They'd lose respect."

Truman's face burned at the allegation, though from rage or shame, he wasn't sure. He couldn't deny the truth in Claber's words. "Respect starts with my men, and that includes you. If you ever do something like that again—" He'd what? Kill him? Claber would know that was an empty threat. "You'll be out."

"Yes, sir," Claber said.

Truman grimaced. His own men found him weak.

CHAPTER 3

Alfred, a white-haired man and by far the oldest in the group, picked up Truman and Claber from the airport late in the evening. Lack of sleep made Truman cranky and irritable. By the time they reached the mansion tucked deep in the Canadian forest, he had a headache the size of Mt. Everest. It pounded like the steady beat of a bass drum.

Barley greeted him as soon as Truman opened the car door, the wet nose nearly knocking him back inside. Barley's entire back half wagged back and forth with the force of his tail.

"Good boy," Truman said, scratching behind his ears. He glanced up to see Grey descending the concrete steps into the garage.

Hey, Boy Scout," Claber sneered at Grey. "How was dog-watching? Earn another merit badge?"

Grey ignored the badgering. "He's glad you're home, Boss. Started whining as soon as he heard the car pull in. Knew it was you."

"The only good thing my father left me," Truman muttered.

Grey shrugged. "Well, the money's nice too."

Truman pressed a hand against his raging head. "Gentlemen, I'm exhausted. Claber, I'm leaving you in charge."

"Take Barley for a walk, Boy Scout," Claber said.

"No." Truman put out a hand, stopping Grey. "Come, boy."

Truman patted his thigh, and Barley leapt to his side. "How are we on food?"

"We could use some food items," Grey admitted.

"Then go get them. I'm sleeping. Do not disturb."

"Out of here, Boy Scout," Claber grumbled.

Truman ignored them. He stumbled into the house and up three flights, pausing only to take a quick drink of tonic and gin. That usually helped. He climbed into bed. Barley jumped on beside him, the weight and smell of the dog comforting. Truman fell asleep before he'd closed his eyes.

At noon Claber walked in and opened the blinds. Sunlight poured over Truman's face, and he winced. "Claber. I did not request a wake-up call."

"Grey just phoned," Claber said, unperturbed. "He can't get up the hill. Says there's a cop staking out the driveway."

Barley jumped off the bed and exited the room, tail wagging the whole time. Truman sat up and directed his attention at Claber. "Where is he now?"

"He kept going. Pretended like that wasn't his stop. But if that cop decides to drive up the mountain..." Claber let the sentence hang.

Truman scowled. "Why is he here? Fayande is supposed to keep them away from here. Isn't that what I'm paying him to do?" Officer Fayande was Truman's inside man to the Montreal police force. It was his job to keep the cops out of Truman's business.

Claber grunted. "Maybe you better remind him."

Truman grabbed the discarded jeans at the foot of the bed and fished through the pockets for his phone. His hand closed around it and he pulled it out, hitting the speed dial for Fayande. Truman didn't worry about Fayande turning him in. Fayande liked the perks of being in The Hand's pocket. Sure beat the policeman wages.

Fayande answered, the French words purring through the

telephone.

Truman interrupted. "Why is one of your men at my doorstep?"

Fayande switched to English in an instant, his voice laced with panic. "One of my men is at your house?"

"No, luckily for you. He is in my driveway."

"Who?"

Truman gritted his teeth. "It's your job to know that, not mine. Get him out of here."

"Right now, I will," Fayande promised. "It—"

Truman hung up. He'd heard all the promises before and wasn't interested. Besides, it would do Fayande good to sit and fret. Truman put his hand on the nightstand and forced himself to his feet. "What's Sanchez's ETA?"

He hadn't heard anything from Sanchez in several hours. The men had killed the guards and rid themselves of the would-be thieves. Killing them didn't sit well with Truman. It wasn't how he operated. At least the men had been criminals and not civilians. *Besides, like Claber said*, Truman consoled himself, *it was us or them.*

"They should be here before dinner," Claber answered. "Spoke with him two hours ago."

"Bring me some black coffee and toast. I'll be in the shower."

———

Grey made it up the hill after the cop disappeared, then unloaded groceries and other essentials into the house. The men grabbed a bite to eat and went back to the game room. Truman followed, listening to their chatter while he checked accounts on his tablet. He skimmed the Mexican news for any information on the killings. They had no suspects. It had to have been the *Carnicero*.

Barley lifted his head from his spot under the pool table and began to growl. A moment later Truman felt the slight tremble of a car passing over the gravel drive. Truman tucked his tablet under an arm and ran up the stairs to the main level, Barley at his heels. He moved down the hall toward the entry way just as Claber exited one of the grand rooms.

"Is it Sanchez?" Truman asked.

"Yes. Just arrived."

Truman grunted. "Why didn't he call ahead?"

"He's on time."

That was true. Still, a head's up was required. "Who's in the driveway?"

"Sanchez with the stolen vehicle. Van's already in the garage."

Truman switched directions, curiosity filling him as he thought about the mystery car. It should provide a few clues.

Sanchez and Allan stood next to the car in the circle drive, deep in conversation. Sanchez leaned against the hood of the dark green BMW, his deep-set eyes shaded by a baseball cap. For a moment the bright sunlight reflecting off the car blinded Truman, and he shielded his eyes. There was something familiar about it.

"Boss." Sanchez pushed off the hood and approached him.

"Everything go right?" Truman studied the sleek sports car in front of him. It didn't look like the normal car used in a robbery. Barley sniffed the tires and then lifted a leg. Truman snapped his fingers. "Barley, down, boy!"

"Where's the boyscout?" Claber snapped and glanced around. "Someone get the dog back in the house!"

Sanchez's eyes darted toward Barley. He made a move as if to grab him.

"Sanchez!" Truman barked. "Tell me what happened."

"We got the jewels. None of our men died."

Truman leaned in the driver's side and inhaled the clean car scent. Nothing his men drove smelled so clean. "Any idea whose car this is?"

"No, boss. We didn't stop to examine it. We got some blood on the exterior... but we took it through a car wash. So it's good now."

"Good thinking." Cleaning up after a homicide wasn't the norm for his men. At least they'd thought on their feet. Truman popped the trunk and went around to the back of the car.

Sanchez and Allan joined him. Sanchez let out a low whistle. "I didn't see that when I was throwing in the bodies. That's a hot piece of metal."

"You didn't notice this blood, either." Truman scowled at the black blood stains on the upholstery, then turned his attention to the weapon in the trunk. He withdrew the long black machine gun, a chill running through him to know how easily his men could've been slaughtered. But who would have such a weapon, and why harass his men? More importantly, why have such a weapon and not use it?

McAllister.

The name popped into Truman's head just as he realized where he'd seen the car before. McAllister had it at a summit in Colorado. McAllister trafficked in illegal weaponry. This was his car.

Truman put the gun down, studying the interior of the rest of the car. He owned several guns and kept his men armed. But most weapons like this one ended up in the hands of tyrants, evil men who lusted after power and had no qualms about murdering hundreds of thousands of people if they stood in their way.

Truman did not condone such behavior. But this weapon sat in the back of a trunk like a gift, a token apology for nearly ruining his raid. And probably several others could be found under the upholstery, in the dash, beneath chairs.

He shut the trunk. "Anyone see you?" he asked without looking at Sanchez.

"Only the dead men."

Truman cringed at the words. "Keep this on the down-low.

Allan, I need an illegal arms dealer. Someone who won't know me. Clear it with me, then take a couple of men and make an exchange. And rip out that upholsery before you sell the car."

"Got it." Allan vanished inside the four-story mansion.

"Sanchez." Truman called back the other man before he could follow Allan. "Stay here. Tell me exactly what happened." Truman stared a moment longer at the dark green car. He had to rid himself of this car, along with the weapons, before McAllister could trace it to him.

CHAPTER 4

Truman's men spread around the game room, plates of sandwiches and chips propped up between card games and beers. Allan and his group should be home in a day from their assignment. The sooner, the better. Truman wanted this whole thing behind him.

Smoke filled the air from various cigarettes and cigars like a sleazy bar from a 1950s mobster movie. Truman pointed his pencil at a road highlighted on the map in front of him. "Put the getaway car here," he said to Claber. "You'll be half a block from the store, but you should be able to make a run for it on foot. I've studied the schematics of the store. Disable the inner cameras as soon as you enter. Stay out of view of the outside ones."

"And this is the only raid we'll do that night?"

"Yes." Truman tapped the pencil eraser on the map. If he had a mole in the local police force, Truman's agents could use their limited power to buy him time, to clear a getaway path for him. But he didn't.

"Target?"

Truman pictured the store in his mind. Located in a strip mall in a small town, it probably didn't have anything worth more than ten grand. His men had thirty seconds from the moment they entered the store. "It'll just be you and Eli. Let's shoot for fifty thousand."

Claber's cell vibrated on the table between them. Truman cocked his head. He didn't give out his own personal number, so anyone wanting to contact him did it through Claber.

Claber shot a look at Truman, his green eyes dark in the smoky air. "McAllister."

Truman's stomach flip-flopped. Sanchez should've sold the weapons by now. Truman couldn't miss the call, though, or it might look like he was avoiding McAllister. "Answer it, quick."

Claber poked a button on the touch screen. "Yes." He raised his eyes to Truman's. "One moment." He handed the phone over.

Truman flipped the map around and ran his pencil over a highway. "McAllister. What can I do for you?"

"Funny you should ask, Truman. I'm not sure that you can, but I thought you should know."

"Know what?" Here it came.

"Some of my men have disappeared."

Truman erased the line he had drawn over the highway. "Deserters?"

"I don't think so. These men were part-timers. They had jobs, families." He paused. "Now they're missing."

Truman gritted his teeth and shot a glare at Claber. He'd killed people who would actually be missed. "Where did they disappear from?"

"They picked up a package for me and were on their way to a delivery. Never made it."

Well, they were idiots to make a pit-stop on my raid. "Could it be the *Carnicero*?"

"Could be, of course, but he usually leaves a crime scene behind."

Too true. The *Carnicero* left his bloody handiwork out in the open, a warning and a promise to dangerous criminals: their turn would come.

"I'm not sure I can help you, then."

McAllister exhaled. "There was a theft at a jewelry store close by where they did their pickup. It had the classic marks of one of yours, so I thought maybe you were in the area."

Truman's neck prickled. Was McAllister fishing? Or did he actually know something? "Me? I never go out on raids."

A soft growl came through the phone. "Your men, Truman."

"Classic marks? It had a hand print?" He hoped not. He'd quit leaving the hand print years ago, preferring to leave cops uncertain whether he was the perpetrator or not.

"No. But it looked like one of your jobs."

A bead of sweat gathered at Truman's hairline. "How strange."

"You didn't do any robberies last week?"

Silently Truman cursed. McAllister hadn't said yet where the crime happened. Now Truman had to play the lazy mastermind. "Busy week. Didn't have a chance."

That was a lie, and he knew McAllister would know it.

"Interesting," McAllister said. "The car's gone too. But I've got a tracer out on it. If it shows up at any dealerships, I'll be notified."

"That's good," Truman said, his face hot. Why hadn't they destroyed the car instead of reselling it? "I hope you find your men."

"And my package. Was worth a pretty penny."

"And your package," Truman echoed.

"We'll be in touch. I'll let you know what I find out."

Truman hung up, not even finding the strength to give a courtesy goodbye. "Claber. We might be in trouble."

In general, Truman left his men alone when they were on a mission. A phone call from him at the wrong time could ruin a raid. So he waited for them to contact him.

But when nightfall came and they still hadn't returned, Truman couldn't wait anymore.

22

He sat at the large oak dining room table at three in the morning, staring at the phone in his hands as if it had betrayed him. Barley slept in front of him, his big yellow head resting on Truman's feet. The dog lifted his head when someone stepped into the room. Truman knew without looking that it was Claber.

"Call it a night," Claber grunted. "I'll stay up and wait."

Truman didn't lift his eyes. "I've tried all three cell phones. No answer."

He waited for words of comfort, for assurances of his own paranoia. He didn't like dealing with the loss and risk that came with the darker side of his profession. As much as he hated to admit it, Claber had a better instinct for it. He needed his opinion. But Claber kept silent.

"Well?" Now Truman looked at him. "What do you think?"

"They may have run into trouble," Claber admitted.

Truman sighed. He wanted a different answer, but he couldn't shake the feeling that Claber was right. "McAllister."

"But how would he know?"

Truman met his eyes, grinding his back teeth together. "We were set up."

"McAllister followed us?"

"Yes. I'm not sure why, but he either wanted to interrupt our raid or he wanted to track our location." Truman waited while Claber digested that information, then said, "We have an agent in Ontario. He's two hours from where Allan's team was going. Contact him. I want to know if there are any reports coming in of accidents or foul play along the route."

"Wouldn't McAllister hide his involvement? Try to lead us off the path by killing them where we wouldn't expect it?"

Killing them. Truman's stomach turned over. That was, after all, the expectation now. His men were probably dead. "I don't think so.

I think McAllister wants us to know he did this. He'll lay it out in the open for us."

"Mocking," Claber said.

"A taunt, for sure," Truman agreed. Anger darkened his insides and twisted there, burning. What did McAllister have against him, anyway?

Revenge his foul and most unnatural murder. Hamlet's father said it best. "Perhaps also an invitation to play."

Claber turned. "I'll make those phone calls."

"I need something to read," Truman said, Shakespeare's haunting words echoing in his mind. In spite of his lack of formal education, the plays of the Bard had captured his attention. Especially the tragedies. The injustice was so poetic.

Barley lifted his head and whined, his large brown eyes mournful. Truman reached down and scratched behind his ears. "Bring me *Hamlet*. No. *Macbeth*." Yes. Betrayals, murders, and three witches. He put his face down on the table and waited for Claber to return.

It seemed only a moment before the table jostled, waking Truman. He blinked blearily and lifted his head. Claber sat next to him and dropped a heavy book on the table.

"Brought you all of Shakespeare. In case you change your mind again."

"Thank you. Anything to report?"

"Yes." Claber's eyes flicked toward a corner of the room, and he smoothed a hand over his buzzed hair. "The Ontario agent investigated for me. Found a two-car accident on a small back road, just south of the rendezvous point. A little greenie and a black sedan."

Truman stood and opened his liquor cabinet. He hovered over the whiskey and chose the Scotch instead. "Cause?"

"Looks like the driver of the green car was shot in the head. He went into a tailspin and took out the sedan when he crashed."

He swallowed back a shot. "Survivors?"

"No, but it wasn't the crash that killed them. All three men in the green car had multiple gunshot wounds."

Truman nodded, feeling his eyes glaze over. Not a big surprise, really. Ever since that conversation last night, he'd felt something coming. Something like this. Truman stood up, drunk with fatigue and worry rather than alcohol.

"One more thing. They didn't find any weapons."

"The machine gun was gone?"

"Gone."

Which begged a question. Had his men enacted the deal before their murders? He tried to dredge up sorrow for their deaths, but the only thing he felt was a prickly fear creeping over his neck.

Truman shook it off. He couldn't do anything right now. "*Macbeth,*" he said. "It's time we got reacquainted."

CHAPTER 5

Truman stayed in bed long after the sun came up. He lay half in and half out of his sheets, keeping the blinds closed and the room dark. His head throbbed and his mouth tasted like cotton.

It was Eli who woke him, his fat lip hanging out over his chin "Boss, sorry to bother you, it's just—"

"What?" Truman snapped, though he was too exhausted to be genuinely irritated.

"It's McAllister." Eli held out Claber's cell phone.

Adrenaline rushed through Truman's veins, and he sat up, heart pumping. He covered the phone and hissed, "Where's Claber?"

"Don't know. But his phone was on the counter, and I answered it."

That protocol needed discussing. But not now. Truman took the phone and said stiffly, "Hello?"

"Truman." McAllister's voice slid across the phone waves like a slimy sea eel. "It appears you lied to me, my friend."

McAllister knew. "There might have been a misunderstanding," Truman hedged.

"No." McAllister's voice turned hard. "I misunderstood nothing. You killed my men, took my car, and stole my guns."

Truman's ire rose. "Then we are partially even," he said. "Since you killed my men."

"Hardly," McAllister growled. "That was fair play. But now the gig's up, and I want my guns back."

"I don't have your guns," Truman said. Even as he said the words, the full meaning hit him in the gut. There'd been no weapons in the car. His men must've sold them before the attack. But then, where was the money? He hadn't seen any deposits for it, and the agent hadn't indicated that the police found it with the bodies. McAllister must have taken it. "As you well know."

"I hope you're lying, Truman," McAllister said, his voice going so soft Truman strained to hear it. "It will not bode well for you if I don't get them back."

"I don't have them," Truman repeated. His mind raced. What could he do to appease McAllister? "Those men attacked one of my raids. I didn't know they were yours. We defended ourselves."

"They were collecting payment, Truman. What you rightfully owe me for our losses in Cancun!"

Truman's heart dropped into a pit in his stomach. McAllister must know how he lured the *Carnicero* to Mexico. But he couldn't know. All Truman had done was leave bread crumbs, really. "What do you mean?"

"You." McAllister's voice rumbled. "You leaked information about our meeting. The Carnicero followed Cisnero to my hotel. We all died. Because of you."

"What makes you think it was me?" Truman tried to sound logical. "You yourself said he's always tracking us."

"Because no one else would be so stupid," McAllister hissed. "You were there days before we were. And you're the only one who doesn't take this seriously."

Truman paused just a moment too long, and he knew it cemented his guilt. "I've had no contact with the *Carnicero*."

"Say what you want, Truman," McAllister growled. "I want my money. I want reimbursement for my dead men. And I want my weapons back. Got that?"

"I'm not—" Truman began, but his defense was cut short.

"Don't make me send you an invoice. I want to exchange money personally. No deposits. I'll be in touch."

The call disconnected and Truman stared in disbelief at the phone in his hand.

"What did he want?" Eli's eyes narrowed. "Something about the *Carnicero*?"

"Nothing to worry about." Truman hadn't seen any money from the sale of the weapons. It might still be in the car. "Take Kessler and the Bennett brothers back to the scene of the accident. Check the car for money. If you find any, deposit it immediately."

Truman waited in the darkened supermarket parking lot, tapping his fingers on the steering wheel in impatience and suspense. He had agreed to meet McAllister's men here at one a.m., but so far they hadn't shown.

The search at the crash site and the impounded vehicle had yielded nothing. No weapons, no money. Which meant someone had taken it. Truman had his suspicions of who that was, and the name started with Mc. He had no proof, however, and pointing fingers might only incriminate him further.

Sanchez snored in the back, and Kessler's head bobbed in the passenger seat while the man struggled to keep his eyes open. McAllister's willingness to allow two of Truman's men to accompany him assuaged some of his fears.

Kessler turned around and whacked Sanchez's leg. "Wake up!"

Sanchez snorted and jerked his head up. "What? What is it?"

"There," Truman said, pointing.

A dark SUV with only its day lights on pulled up beside Truman. A beefy man emerged from the passenger side and opened the back door. He stood next to it, arms crossed, waiting.

Truman grimaced. He hadn't planned on going anywhere. He didn't see an easy way out of this, though, so he pocketed his keys and emerged from his Ferrari. "Where's McAllister? I thought he had something to tell me."

"He does. Get in the car."

Truman leaned back against the low profile of his car and folded his arms. "You must think I'm crazy."

The beefy man cracked his knuckles and glared at Truman. Sanchez got out on the other side of the car, followed by Kessler.

"I have my orders, Truman. I need you all with me. McAllister is waiting." The man sneered, his eyes following Truman's men as they circled the vehicle and flanked him. "And you know how he hates to be kept waiting."

Before Truman could react, the beefy man shot out a fist, hitting Kessler in the jaw. He fell against the car, and Sanchez threw a right hook into the neck of the man pummeling Kessler.

"Enough!" Truman shouted, coming between them. "I'm pretty sure McAllister needs me in a cooperative mood." He gestured toward the open door.

The beefy man stood up straight, rolling a shoulder and popping his neck. "Get in." He stood at the door like an avenging footman. One hand swung toward the car's interior.

"But boss—" Sanchez started.

Truman cut him off. "Just get in the car."

The beefy guy waited for him and his men to get in, then closed the door and returned to the front.

"All right," Truman said as the car peeled away from the parking lot. "Where are we going?"

"You'll see when we get there," the driver said.

Something large whacked Truman in the back off his head,

hard. His vision swam and then went black.

When Truman came to, he sat in a chair with his hands tied behind his back, his head pounding painfully. He could see nothing in front of him except darkness, but he sensed he wasn't alone.

He ran his tongue along the inside of his mouth, trying to moisten it. "Where am I?" he croaked.

A single light bulb in front of Truman clicked on. It swayed, leaving little purple and black dots in his line of vision. It also illuminated McAllister as he leaned forward in a chair across from Truman.

"Welcome."

Truman stared back at the man. The pain in his head made it difficult to think. "Is this how you treat all your guests?"

"Sorry for the less-than-gracious accommodations. You are, at this point, more foe than friend. But perhaps we can change that."

Truman's chest tightened. He didn't want to be on the bad side of any of these mercenaries. "Where are my men?"

"On either side of you." McAllister gestured.

Truman swiveled his head, and he realized two other chairs backed up against his. Sanchez and Kessler were not only tied up, but gagged. He couldn't make out their faces enough to see if they were awake. "What do you want?"

"Simple. My weapons, and reimbursement for my losses."

"I don't have them." And he didn't have any money for McAllister, either. None he was willing to give up.

McAllister leaned closer, a gleam in his black eyes. "Millions," he said, his breath rank with the smell of cigarette smoke. "Those weapons were worth millions if sold into the right hands. Black market. But you wouldn't know that. You wouldn't even know who to sell them to. So where are they?" He pulled a gun from his pocket and caressed the mouth of the barrel.

Truman knew a threat when he saw one. "I don't know."

"But you saw them." McAllister loaded a bullet into the chamber with a sharp click. "Didn't you?"

"I saw them. They never left the car. Unless you know otherwise." As far as he knew, Truman was telling the truth. Maybe the weapons were never sold. "If they weren't there after the car crash, I don't know where they went. Maybe someone is not being honest with you." That might be true, too. Because something was missing, whether it was the weapons or the money. And Truman didn't have it.

"Michael," McAllister whispered.

Michael? What did that mean?

Truman only had a moment to wonder before a man stepped from the shadows and dropped a pillowcase over his head. A moment later his chair flipped over so that Truman lay on his back, hands crushed between him and the concrete floor.

Water gushed over his face, seeping into the cloth around his nose and mouth. Truman gasped for breath, but only liquid filled his mouth. He inhaled and snorted against the burn as water gushed into his nostrils.

He couldn't breathe. His heart beat erratically, and his hands pulled against the rope holding them, grabbing at the chair as he struggled for air. He tossed his head to and fro, trying to shake the pillowcase off, until someone grasped him in a vice-grip and held him still. Truman bellowed, but more water entered his mouth. He grew lightheaded and banged his head against the chair.

The chair righted and the cloth came off. Truman sputtered, sucking air into his lungs, rasping against the ache in his chest.

"We were saying," McAllister continued as if nothing had happened. "Where are those weapons?"

31

McAllister will kill me.

With that realization, Truman's composure crumpled. "Listen." He tried to shout the word, but his raw throat only managed a stage whisper. "I'm being completely honest. We don't have—"

McAllister flicked his finger and Truman was on his back again, pillowcase shoved over him. Again he tossed his head until someone held him still. He sputtered, a soundless scream fighting over the streaming water.

When they sat him up, Truman hung his head, staring at the ground and gasping as water ran down his chin and nose. He waited. This was McAllister's game.

"Now. Where are those weapons?"

Truman didn't answer. Water pooled on the concrete beneath his feet.

"Truman. Where are they?"

The Hand. He was The Hand. Anger and fear surged together into a desperate wave of defense, and his head bobbed up. "I don't know!" His hoarse voice echoed in the room, which must've been bigger than he thought. "My men are dead! I never received payment for the weapons, and I don't have them!"

"Ah." A satisfied smile drew up the corners of McAllister's mouth. "But you did take them. Now we're getting somewhere." He templed his fingers and pressed the tips to the goatee on his chin. "I guess that means you owe me."

"Yes," Truman whispered. "I owe you." *Just let us out of here*, he thought, *and we'll see about who owes who.*

"I would say you owe me quite a bit. So let's cut a deal. Your life —for ten million."

Truman sputtered. Ten *million*? He would have to triple—no, quadruple—his number of raids, make an effort to bring in the big bucks, cut his men's pay, risk losing his moles, all in the name of making this money.

"You think that's a lot?" The smile still played on McAllister's face. "Let's add things up. You led the *Carnicero* to us in Mexico. I lost men and merchandise. Two million. You shot my men. You might not think they were worth much, but they were to me. And now I'm supporting their families. So one million for both of them. Then there's the car. Not my nicest vehicle, but a good car. Fifty grand. But then we've also got the issue of the weapons." His eyes flashed in the darkness. "I could've gotten almost a million for each, and I had five of them."

"That's only eight million," Truman protested.

"But we're here, aren't we?" McAllister growled. "I had to search for my men. I had to contact you. Then I had to drag you out here, wasting my time and yours, so we could come to an agreement. My time is valuable." His hand twitched. "Wouldn't you agree?"

Truman's eyes strayed to the man behind McAllister's left shoulder. He gave a nod.

McAllister struck him in the side of the head again. "Answer me!" He screamed.

"Yes!" Truman screamed back. His vision swam again, and he could hardly focus on the man in front of him.

McAllister seated himself. "Glad we are in agreement. Therefore I added on another two million. Call it inflation, call it service charge, call it manual labor." He put his hands on his knees and leaned close enough to Truman for their noses to touch. "Or call it revenge. But that is my price. Your life is included there. Take it or leave it."

Truman couldn't make that money. But the other option wasn't really viable. Literally. Somehow he had to come up with it. "How long?"

"I'll give you one month."

One month was hardly enough time, but Truman knew better than to reason with a madman. McAllister had set the bar high so Truman would fail. The man would like nothing better than to see him fall. "All right. I'll do it."

"So glad we could come to an arrangement." He stood and stretched, motioning his thug to untie Truman.

Truman relaxed his fists, trying not to show how he trembled.

The man untied Kessler next, then moved on to Sanchez. Truman met Sanchez's eyes, gave him a small nod.

"Oh, one more thing, Truman," McAllister said, his tone conversational. "I forgot to mention what will happen if you fail."

Truman didn't even want to know. He rubbed his wrists. "What?"

"I will hunt you, Truman." He pulled out his gun and leveled it at Sanchez, who had barely stood up. "I will take you down." He hot Sanchez's right foot. Sanchez shrieked around his gag and 'abbed his foot, stumbling on the left one.

"One man," McAllister continued, shooting Sanchez in the left gh.

"Stop!" Truman shouted, making a move toward Sanchez even as the man collapsed on the concrete, moaning and writhing in agony.

"At a time," McAllister finished, shooting Sanchez in the head.

The last gunshot echoed in the room, made more poignant by the silence that followed. Sanchez lay still, his bloody remains speckling the gray floor. Truman stared, a nameless horror building in the pit of his stomach and spreading to his pounding head.

This wasn't an arrangement. It was a threat. It wasn't a debt, it was a ransom.

"There was no need for that," Truman said, finally finding his voice. The words came out calm, surprising himself.

"Consider it an object lesson," McAllister replied evenly. "Just in case you thought about running, or cheating, or anything less than fulfilling our bargain."

"Of course," Truman said, as if killing his man were nothing out of the ordinary. "Now let us go, before I have no one left to help me collect your money."

McAllister chuckled and gestured to his thug. "Blindfold Truman and get him out of here."

Truman stiffened. "Just me?" He cursed himself for not seeing through McAllister's plan. This was why he hadn't made Truman come alone.

"We'll keep your friend here." McAllister stepped up to Kessler and put a hand on his shoulder. "As collateral."

Truman met Kessler's eyes and then dropped his gaze. He had no intention of losing this man's life to McAllister as well. But he wasn't certain he could succeed.

No more words were exchanged while Truman was blindfolded, but none were needed. The consequence of failing sat heavily in the air, ringing in Truman's ears as they marched out to the car.

CHAPTER 6

Claber gathered the men into the study the moment Truman got back to the mansion. Truman knew he looked like a wreck, but he had to explain the situation to them, and it had to be now.

He thrust a small dagger into the surface of his wooden desk while he waited for the men, then yanked it out only to thrust it in again.

"This is all that's here," Claber said, closing the door behind him. Several men were away on raids, but about seven remained at the mansion.

For a brief moment Truman wanted to tell them all to remember who they'd been before they came to him, where they'd lived, and to go back to that life.

But that wouldn't be good for him, and the selfless moment passed.

"We're going to make some changes." He sat on the corner of his desk and threw the dagger into the opposite corner of the flat wood surface. "We'll be increasing the number of raids we do each week."

"Each week?" Hastings echoed. "I thought once a week was risky!"

"Not anymore." Truman waited a moment to let his annoyance fade a bit. Hastings reminded him of a high school student. "We're also going to start hitting a new venue."

Murmurs ran around the group. Long had Truman made it clear that he stole jewelry, and nothing else. For him to change that proved how desperate he was.

A whisper rippled through his group, until the older Bennett brother, Derek, had the guts to ask, "Why the change?"

Truman pressed his lips together, growing irritated. He shouldn't have to explain his every thought. Most knew he'd met with McAllister, but they didn't need to know more than that."It's time to expand. If you want out, be my guest. Don't expect any more payments, and remember that being on your own is on your own. No protection."

He let those words sink in for a moment. Then Grey asked, "Where are Kessler and Sanchez?"

Irony. On the heels of threatening to take away protection, he now had to admit that he didn't have much to offer. Truman cleared his throat. "Kessler stayed behind with McAllister. He had some complaints. He'll be back soon." There. Let it seem like it was voluntary, that he and Kessler made some kind of agreement.

The silence dragged on too long, and Grey cleared his throat. "And Sanchez?"

Sanchez. An image of the shot-up body flashed before Truman's eyes. If he told them, he would either have a mutiny or people second-guessing his every decision. On the other hand, if he lied, they would find out soon. And then all their trust in him would vanish.

"Sanchez is dead." Truman hardened his face and met each man's eyes. They wouldn't know if it was him or McAllister who pulled the trigger, but it would breed a healthy fear among the men.

Truman leaned forward, plucking his dagger out of the desk and cleaning his fingernails with it. "Here's the new plan. As often as we can spare men, we'll have raids going on. And we're going for bigger items. Museums. Special exhibits. It's going to take some training, but it will work. A good change of pace. So you know the plan. Let's get to work, boys."

The men filed out of the room, all except Claber. He ran a hand over his buzzed head. "I've gone over all the pictures I took in Cancun. I printed several that could be our man. Maybe the *Carnicero*, or maybe one of the other shadows that follow him."

"Excellent. Give them to me. I'll have Fayande take a look at them, see if he can ID anyone."

"Will do."

———

Five in the morning, and Truman lounged in an extra-large leather chair in the game room. Barley had taken up his usual spot on top of Truman's toes, the sixty-pound body of the dog warming his legs and calming his nerves. He reached down, absentmindedly massaging behind his ears. Several members of his team were still up. Cold hot wings and sandwiches piled up on the counter.

The facade of normalcy was complete. It wasn't unusual for many people to be up this time of night, especially when waiting on the results of a raid. The smells, the low lights, the food, the alcohol. But there was the catch. Usually, Truman nursed a beer while he played. Tonight, he cradled his whiskey. His fingers moved robotically across the dog's head, unable to keep up with the anxiety that spidered through his chest and crawled over his neck.

The others were tense, as well. This was a new game they were playing. Eyes kept lifting from their card games to dart to the clock on the wall, or risk a glance at Truman before turning away. Tensions were high. Tonight should show them that they could handle the change.

At least, if everything went well. He watched their silent card games and was grateful they didn't know the real stakes.

Truman had sent Claber on this raid. Too much rested on this one to trust it to someone else. He, one of the Bennett brothers, and Christof had traveled to the Washington DC area the day before. Truman had carefully selected a mid-profile art museum. It had security, but not as intense as the more famous museums. And yet if he managed to steal just one original art piece, he'd be a tenth of the way to paying off his debt.

Of course his men wouldn't take just one. They would go for a collection, something worth ten or fifteen million. Shouldn't be too hard.

Yet Truman had never gone after something so valuable. It wasn't in his job description. He acted confident in front of the men, but his hands shook with agitation. How good of a thief was he? Robbing a jewelry store took some skill and wit and speed. But what about an art museum?

The phone rang, startling Barley, who ran off. Probably under his desk, the chicken. Truman consulted his wristwatch. A quarter after five. The raid was set to start just before three a.m. Nearly two and a half hours to complete the job. Too long. "Yes?"

"Boss." Claber's voice came through, loud and clear. Wind or something noisy buzzed in the background.

"What?" Truman strode from the game room, moving out of hearing from the others. "Are you done?"

Claber heaved a sigh. "Yeah, we're done. We failed. We couldn't do it."

Truman gripped the phone tighter. He'd half expected this outcome, but still, it couldn't be right. "What do you mean?" He glanced toward the game room, not wanting anyone else to overhear. "There was so much resting on this! You couldn't fail!"

"I'm sorry." Claber's voice remained steady. "We barely got away. We disabled the alarm, as usual, but there must've been another. Maybe when we took the painting off the wall." His voice rose in pitch. "And the paintings were heavy. It took all three of us to carry one. We heard the guards approaching, running. We tried to run with the painting, but in the end we had to ditch it. Like I said, we barely got away. We hid the van in a darkened house across the street. The cops showed up just as we piled in, so we stayed inside for two hours, laying low with the doors locked. They came by, shone their lights in, but they didn't see us. Not that it would matter; we didn't get the painting. Things calmed down, so we're on the road again."

Truman raked a hand through his short hair. He felt like an idiot. There must've been a way for him to foresee this. "You wore gloves and masks?"

"Of course."

"Security cameras?"

"We cut that part of the electrical grid. But they might've had back-up power, seeing as how we triggered an alarm somewhere. Still, we were in black. Only our flashlights would've been visible."

"No one's following you?"

"No one," Claber confirmed.

"How many guards did you take out?"

"Just two, the ones in the front. We gassed them. One struggled, but he went under without being struck. So no injuries."

Truman nodded to himself. Killing McAllister's men had started all this trouble. It wouldn't happen again.

Even as he thought it, a desperate itch started under his ribcage and worked its way up. Perhaps it wasn't possible anymore to avoid confrontations. His men carried weapons. If they had fired on a guard, could they have bought enough time to escape with a painting?

Doubtful. Truman sighed again. "Find a motel and stay down

there. I'll rethink our next steps. We might have to change our tactics a bit."

"A bit?" Claber echoed. "Boss, we're way behind. We're playing like children in a battlefield. If we're going to play in the big league, we need to act like big leaguers."

It was the closest Claber had ever come to chastising Truman, and he bristled. Yet Claber was right. He couldn't make the money he needed without breaking a few arms. And that meant stepping out of the comfortable mold he'd made for himself.

CHAPTER 7

"Here's the new plan," Truman said, his voice echoing over the speaker function of his phone. He leaned nearer the microphone. "Is everyone listening?"

"We're all here," Claber said.

"Here, Boss," Grey said, his words distorted by the speaker on Claber's cell.

"Here," Eli echoed.

"All right." Truman inhaled through his nostrils.

Claber's group had stopped in a cheap motel somewhere in Virginia, but they wouldn't be there long. "I've made some decisions," Truman continued. "We're going back to jewelry. It's what we know best. But not just any jewelry. Museum pieces."

A bed creaked on the other side of the phone, and Truman knew they weren't thrilled by the idea. They'd probably prefer never to step foot into a museum again.

"Don't worry." Truman spoke before anyone could object. "Even you can do these ones." The insult in his words would be like fire to their egos, propelling them forward to the next task. "These museums aren't as protected. I'm sending you to Texas."

"Texas?" Eli asked, surprised.

"Houston, to be exact," Truman said. "There's a special art exhibit this week only. The Swan Lake necklace. Worth almost two million." He'd found the special exhibit after just a few internet searches. Then it hadn't taken much to bribe a contact into visiting the museum and scouting out the security. Between the expensive exhibit and the lesser security, the Houston museum was the best combination for his men.

He heard scribbling on paper, and then Claber asked, "What's security like?"

"Tight, but not too. I've got a rear entry point with only two guards. Should be really quick. If you're lucky, they'll be in another part of the museum. If you're not, gas them. It shouldn't be too hard."

"One of us can even create a distraction," Eli said.

"We got this," Claber said, repressed excitement in his voice. "When do we leave?"

"In the morning. Give yourselves two days. I want you there by Wednesday at the latest. Get the necklace, then head west to the Rockies. Come up into Canada through our Montana route."

"The Montana way?" Grey interrupted, his voice closer to the phone. "But the museum's in Texas."

Truman rolled his eyes. Better if Grey stuck to sewing and cooking. "The police won't be searching for suspects that far away. Get across the border as quick as possible. No stops, got it? Get back here with that necklace. That's all that matters." Two million. That would go a long way toward his debt. At least it would be something to show McAllister, an indication that he took this threat seriously.

"Yes, sir," Claber confirmed. "We'll be back within the week."

"I'll text you the address to the museum. Oh, and Claber," Truman paused. "This mission cannot fail. You have to get that necklace. Do whatever it takes."

"Understood," Claber said.

Truman knew Claber had been chomping at the bit for some time now, wanting something bigger than ring-napping.

Well, he was going to get it.

———

"I have a possible identification on one person from the photographs you gave me," Fayande said, his voice particularly nasal this time of the morning.

Truman switched the phone to his other shoulder and did another pull-up. Sweat dripped down his chin, dampening the white tank he wore. "Go on."

"We have him on our wanted list as well. We have identified two aliases for him. Gregorio and Alejandro."

Truman dropped into a chair, breathing hard and trying not to choke on the musty basement air. "Why is he on your list?"

"Possession of illegal firearms, murder. Resisting arrest, falsifying documents. The last photograph we got was at an airport three years ago. The passport he used at that time said he was Alejandro, from Mexico. Mexican authorities gave us the name Gregorio da Silva and said he is Brazilian. Brazilian authorities have never heard of him. Our trail ended there."

It was a very good lead. "Send me a copy of the photo. We'll track him down."

"I am emailing it to you now."

Truman reloaded his email several times before the message appeared. It took over three minutes for the jpeg to open. He was ready to give the stupid machine to Barley as a chew toy when the image finally loaded. It was out of focus but clear enough. The man's face was in profile as he crossed the street, jaw loose as if chewing gum. Tall, Latino, with a trim black beard framing his face. Late forties.

Could this be him? Could this be the *Carnicero*? Truman copied the email to Claber and gave him a call. "Take a look at this image I'm sending you. What do you remember about this one? He might be the man we're looking for."

Claber checked in with Truman an hour before the raid in Houston. He had orders to call again as soon as they completed the raid, and Truman knew he would. This time, instead of waiting in the game room, surrounded by emotionally distressed men, he stayed up in his bedroom. He kept a full liquor cabinet there anyway.

At one in the morning, the eastern Canadian air felt crisp and humid, with a bite to the mild breeze. Truman stood on the small balcony and shivered. The chill kept his mind clear, despite the whiskey he'd been ingesting since Claber's call. He looked down over the dark pine trees swaying back and forth over the mountainside and swayed with them as he tipped the bottle back again. Even in the day time, Truman couldn't see the gravel road that led to the highway below. At night, not even his men liked to drive up the mountain. Certainly no one else came to visit.

Privacy. He thrived on it. He appreciated the camaraderie he had with his men, and even felt familial ties with some of them. But when it came down to it, he preferred to be alone. That was when he did his best thinking. It was also when he could pretend he lived a normal life.

He closed his eyes, remembering a time when he hadn't known the pressures his father would place on him. He had assumed, like everyone else, that he'd go to college, get a job, get married, and have a family.

High school changed all that. His father suddenly appeared in his life and began grooming him for his inheritance, and friends' houses became training grounds for thievery. Friendships didn't last long after that, and neither did school.

Not that it mattered. His father had always known he'd uproot Truman from his civilian lifestyle and plunk him in the middle of the woods to take over his organization.

Except... Truman hadn't done it right. He never wanted to be a criminal mastermind. And yet, he had never denounced it either. He admitted being unwilling to give up the luxurious lifestyle he had, the gluttonous amounts of food and riches and travels. He prided himself on his fine tastes, the collection of sculptures and busts that adorned his house, the hand-painted murals.

If only the loneliness didn't feel so forced. It was one thing to choose to be isolated; it was another to have no one to pass the time with. His men did not fill the void in his life.

The cell phone on the night stand rang, vibrating until it fell onto the floor. Truman turned, leaving the balcony and crossing the room in three giant steps. Claber. "Well?" He pressed the phone against his cheek and lowered his voice. "Did you get it?"

"We did," Claber said. Triumph tinged both words, punctuating each with emphasis. "We have the necklace."

Grey and Eli whooped loudly in the background. Truman nodded. One necklace wouldn't cancel out his debt, but in the hands of the right buyer, it was a step in the right direction. "How did it go?"

"Fine. It went fine."

Claber's voice changed, and Truman knew he wasn't telling everything. "What went wrong?"

"Nothing went wrong." Claber hesitated. "I did what you said to do. Whatever it takes."

"Meaning?" Truman demanded, not sure he really wanted to know.

"We had to take extra measures, that's all. We gassed the first two security guards without any problems. But another came around the bend right as we were leaving. We didn't expect him."

Truman swore. He hadn't thought the other guards would venture so far from their posts. "Did he see you?"

"He pulled his gun out."

Truman exhaled, his heart rate slowing. "But you got away? And no one was hurt?" At least the raid wasn't wrecked.

"None of us were hurt."

Truman tensed as he realized the way Claber had phrased that. "Was someone else hurt?"

"It was him or us, Boss. So I shot him."

Another murder. Truman cursed and slammed his bottle onto the table. Was there nothing else Claber could've done? A line from *The Life of Timon of Athens* came to his mind: *He commands us to provide and give great gifts, And all out of an empty coffer.* Claber only had what Truman had given him to work with, and that had proven faulty. "Were you seen?"

"The van, maybe. But we took out the plate light and blacked out the registration. We'll fix it tomorrow."

"Where are you now?"

"Heading for New Mexico. We're running high right now." Indeed, there was an exuberance in Claber's voice that Truman rarely heard. "We'll stop to rest closer to morning."

"Keep your eye out for cops," Truman instructed. His network in the US was strained, and more than likely he wouldn't be able to bail them out of trouble if the police found them.

"We will," Claber said cheerfully.

"Good job," Truman said, but the words felt remote. A hollowness filled his chest. He had the necklace. But at what cost?

What was he becoming?

The ringing phone woke Truman from a deep slumber. His eyes refused to open and his head throbbed like someone had stuffed it with cotton.

The phone stopped, and he hauled his pillow over his head. Birds whistled their early morning greeting outside, and he groaned. Details of the night before came back to him. Staying up until three a.m., the successful raid, stealing the Swan Lake necklace.

The phone started up again, dancing its way toward the edge of the nightstand. Why would Claber be calling this early?

He reached out and grabbed the phone. Restricted. A knot of trepidation formed in his gut. Claber would not call from a restricted number. But nobody else should even *have* his number. "Hello?"

"Good morning, Truman." McAllister's voice purred through the line, cheerfully sinister. "How are you today?"

The knot hardened into a cold rock. Truman wanted to ask how McAllister had gotten his number, but it was a moot point. He had the number, and it only showed that he was resourceful.

Truman's house, tucked up in the pine-covered foothills of Montreal, was entirely self-sustaining. A well outside provided water. Generators created the electricity necessary for lighting, heating, and cooling. He had no land-line, only cell phones, and those were pay-as-you-go. No one could track him. No internet, either, except the hotspot he got on his phone. While records of the house existed, there was nothing to tie it back to him.

The message was clear: it wouldn't be long before McAllister tracked down Truman's residential address, as well.

These thoughts flashed through Truman's head in an instant. He cleared his throat, careful not to betray his fear. "Same to you. Not a social call, I assume."

"Correct." Heavy breathing filled the phone line. "Do you hear that? It's a friend of yours. Say hello."

Kessler. Truman heard the muffled sounds of fearful whimpers. He gritted his teeth. "I'm getting you your money. Last night my men stole a two-million dollar necklace. I—"

"Two-million?" McAllister interrupted, sounding amused. "You owe me ten."

"Yes, I know." Truman spat the words out. "This is just the beginning. I'll have all the money soon." He let out a careful breath. "I might need a little more than a month."

"You don't have it." McAllister paused. "However... is the necklace on you?"

"No, not yet. My men will be here in three days."

"Give me the necklace as soon as you get it. I'll keep it as a down payment and extend you another four weeks."

Truman's heart thudded in his ears. Two months still wasn't very much. "I'll do it."

"Good." Something slammed loudly, making Truman jump. A high-pitched, muffled scream echoed in the background. "Your man here is counting on you. He's already given his *hand* in your defense."

Hot rage dipped through Truman's mind, blinding him for a moment. If he could reach through the phone and pull McAllister's throat out, he would. He hung up the phone, his whole body trembling with fury.

CHAPTER 8

Truman couldn't sleep after McAllister's call. He went on a jog with Barley, letting some tension in his joints seep into the cold September air. He finished his jog at the shooting range just east of the house and fired a few rounds. He didn't have an endless supply of ammo, though, and it occurred to him that he might need it.

Chilled by the thought of a bloodbath, he went down to the basement and lifted weights. The odor of mildew and rust overwhelmed his nostrils, and his eyes wandered over the mess in the room. Trash piled up in the corners. Rust decorated the pipes and sinks. The basement stank of wet and decay.

Claber's call at noon was a welcome distraction. "We're in Utah," he said. "Heading for the Montana border."

"Perfect," Truman said into the phone. He entered the kitchen and scowled at the food and trash littering the room. Did nobody clean up after themselves? Sometimes Grey was far more beneficial at home than on raids. He opened the fridge and tossed half of the contents into a trash bag. "Wait until nightfall or our agent might not be working." They had safely crossed the border many times, even if the border patrol didn't include one of Truman's men. But with a theft as important as the Swan Lake necklace on board, Truman preferred to play it safe.

"We will."

The rest of the day passed in a monotonous silence. Truman spent most of it outside with Barley, finding the emptiness of the house oppressive and stifling. He didn't go inside until it got too dark to see.

Toward midnight the phone rang, waking Truman from where he slept at the foot of his bed. Claber again. Truman cleared his throat and answered. "Yes."

"Boss?" Not Claber. Eli's voice came across the line, high-pitched and whiny. Unusual for Eli.

Truman pinched the bridge of his nose and closed his eyes. "What is it, Eli?" Something couldn't have gone wrong so soon. Not now.

"We had, um, uh, a slight mishap."

Truman's lower lip curled into a snarl. "What? What happened?"

"We had to kidnap these four girls that were spying on us."

It took a full minute for the words to sink in. Girls. Spying. Kidnap. "You did what?" he shouted.

"Well, they were—" The phone went dead.

Truman pulled it away from his ear and stared at it. Signal lost. He waited a few minutes for Eli to call back, but he didn't. They must be in a dead zone. There were half a dozen of those between Montana and Canada.

Rattled, Truman lay back on his bed. He tried to summon the hypnosis of sleep, but thoughts tumbled around his mind, trying to make sense of Eli's brief sentences. Kidnap? Girls? How? Why? What were his men doing with them?

Truman sat up and opened the nightstand drawer. As it should be, the whiskey bottle lay on its side, silent and inviting. Truman took a big swig, then another. Kidnap. Spying. Four girls.

He was a jewel thief. Not a kidnapper. This was not part of the game.

He took several more gulps before collapsing face down on the bed, passed out.

Claber didn't call all the next day, and Truman resisted the urge to check on them. The only words Truman had for his second-in-command were furious and condemning. Claber knew better. How could he let something like this happen? Kidnapped girls. Every cop in the nation would be looking for them.

It took some effort for Truman to scan the American newscast on his tablet. Finally, with the right combination of words, he found an APB, put out by the Idaho Falls Police Department.

"Four girls, disappearing from the Idaho Falls mall after ten p.m."

The mall? Why were his men at the mall?

He studied the girls' names and bios again. Just a couple of teenagers. His heart sank. What was he supposed to do with them? He couldn't very well just let them go. But they couldn't be here.

The sun still hung high in the sky around three p.m. when Sanders burst in. "Boss. They're here."

By now all his men knew the kidnapped girls were coming. Truman kept his face stern and followed Sanders back downstairs. Men crowded around the windows, anxious to get a peek.

Stepping out onto the porch, Truman watched the black van pull into the circle drive. Claber emerged from the passenger side. His eyes darted toward Truman, then turned away before they made contact. Truman grimaced. Claber knew this was a bad situation. How could he have allowed it to happen?

Claber straightened his shoulders, his green shirt tightening over his deltoids, and palmed a baseball bat. With one hand, he threw open the cargo doors.

Truman didn't move, but he couldn't deny the curiosity. What kind of girls were these? Did they want trouble?

A Hispanic girl emerged first, her gaze roving over the house before landing on him. She stared, brown eyes wide, before lowering her gaze. Behind her a taller redhead stepped out. Her face swiveled left and right as if she couldn't control the movement. The third girl looked younger than the other two, even younger in real life than in the photo attached to the APB. Her shoulders hunched over and she gripped her forearms, never once lifting her eyes from the gravel path beneath her feet.

Something about her seemed familiar. Truman studied her as they neared before realizing that a fourth girl hadn't come out. He waited, but Eli closed up the van and followed behind the girls, his fat lip jutting out even further than usual.

Truman jerked his head, trying to catch Claber's eye. But Claber didn't look at him as he led the girls into the house.

Grey came up last, and Truman pulled him aside. "What's going on, Grey?"

Grey cleared his throat, eyes darting about as if seeking a hiding place. "We just did what Claber said. Honest, boss."

In other words, Grey wasn't taking credit. "There's only three." Truman let the statement fall and hang there, waiting for an explanation.

Grey coughed. "The other girl's dead."

"Dead?" Truman asked sharply.

"I didn't really see." Grey shook his head. "I was in the van." He stood there a moment, waiting for more questions. But Truman could see Grey didn't have the answers. He released the other man's arm.

"Keep Barley out of sight," he ordered. The girls might attach themselves to the dog, or worse, he to them.

Grey bobbed his head and scurried away, reminding Truman of a mouse evading a predator.

Truman caught up to the girls and Claber, listening as the bigger man snapped out threats and innuendo. Truman stayed back, allowing them to talk unimpeded by his presence. Claber led them all the way to the fourth floor, and then yanked the drop-down ladder to the ground, revealing the attic access.

The small blond girl gripped the ladder and started into the attic, and with a jolt of recognition, Truman knew her.

"Becca." He breathed the name to himself. But it wasn't Becca. It couldn't be. Becca was dead.

Still, something about her so reminded him of Becca that he couldn't remove his gaze from her. He found he'd stepped closer without meaning to. He clenched his fist to keep himself from reaching out and touching her, just to see if she was real. Was her hair as soft as he remembered? Did her nose still crinkle when she smiled? Did her eyes sparkle as if lit from the inside?

Truman shook his head. "Claber."

Claber turned, still not meeting his eyes. "Yes, boss?" he grunted.

"I'll take it from here."

The girl finished scrambling up the ladder, disappearing into the attic.

Claber cast one last glance at them. "Take a rest, ladies. Maybe tonight you'll have company!" His grin faded as he met Truman's eyes for the first time, and then he clomped down the hall.

Anger boiled just beneath the surface of Truman's calm exterior. Perhaps giving the man so much power had been a mistake. "No company today, girls." He studied the two cowering against the ladder. He wished he could reassure them, tell them they wouldn't be hurt. But they might be. They hadn't exactly walked into a butterfly palace. "This is my house, and I'm in charge. Do exactly what I tell you, and I won't hurt you." Which was true, at least. "I don't know about Claber, though. And he's my second-in-command. He'll be in charge of you for most of the time. Up, now. Go on."

Truman waited until they were all in the attic, and then he closed the trapdoor and latched it from the outside. His head pounded. He gritted his teeth and marched downstairs.

He went all the way down to the game room, where the murmur of voices dropped off the moment he entered. Truman stepped up to the bar and poured a glass of whiskey before turning around. All eyes dropped to their tables, laptops, card games, or whatever entertained them, under his scrutiny. Truman noticed the men centered themselves around Claber, Grey, and Eli. He scowled. So his men would know the scoop before him. He couldn't lose face in front of them.

"Claber." The man stood, but Truman waved him down. "This house needs to be cleaned. Top to bottom. You're in charge of those girls tomorrow. Put them to work by six. Keep them busy or they'll cause trouble. And then I want you to report to my office. Seven a.m." Yes, that was a bit early, but Truman wanted Claber to feel his ire.

"Sir?" Claber furrowed his brow. "How can I be in charge of the girls and in your office at the same time?"

Truman stared at him, letting the question linger in the air just until the silence grew heavy. "You delegate." Turning, he grabbed up the rest of the bottle of whiskey and went upstairs, just in case his bedroom supply was running low.

CHAPTER 9

True to his orders, Truman heard Claber's steps stomp past his room and toward the attic entrance a few minutes before six the next morning. Truman stared at his reflection in the bathroom mirror, half of his face still covered in shaving cream. He tried to discern the other pair of steps with Claber, but he couldn't identify the person.

"Just let Claber handle this," he muttered. But images of Becca flashed in his head, and he couldn't let it alone. Toweling off his face, he headed upstairs after Claber.

Claber and Sanders stood a few feet from the stairwell, close to the attic entry. The ladder was down, and Truman surmised that they were waiting for the girls to descend. He approached the two men, earning a nod from Claber. The girls talked softly in the attic, and then jean-clad legs started down the ladder. The brunette. Behind her came the redhead. Truman stepped closer so he could overhear them.

"Maybe now we can escape," the redhead whispered. "Watch for the weaknesses of the house."

Of course, girls who thought themselves clever enough to spy on other people's business would assume they could find a way to escape. Truman crossed his arms over his chest. "There are none."

The girl let out a cry and almost lost her balance, catching herself before she fell off the ladder. She turned and stared at him, green eyes wide. The thought struck Truman that she was very pretty, but that didn't matter. The first lesson here would be respect. "Where would you go? To the police?" The Montreal police wouldn't touch them with a ten-foot pole, not once they knew The Hand was involved with them. "Enough. For now, you're my prisoners."

The last girl, the young blond one, started down the ladder. Truman's eyes lifted to her, almost against his will, and he worked hard to keep his face straight. Becca. Just seeing her made a warm feeling erupt in his chest. He forced himself to look back at the redhead, and he pointed at Claber and Sanders. "Go."

They scurried away, making an obvious effort to step around him. Truman ran his hand over his cleanly shaved chin. What had he gotten into?

At exactly seven o'clock, a knock sounded on the heavy wooden door to Truman's office. "Come in," Truman said, settling himself on top of the desk. This he couldn't wait to hear.

Claber came in. Truman gestured for him to close the door. "Well? What's your explanation?"

Claber grimaced. "We didn't mean for it to happen."

"Granted." Truman leaned forward, putting a hard tone in his voice. "But it did. And I want to know why. Why are there three girls in my house? And what happened with the fourth?"

Silence answered, and a bad feeling settled in Truman's gut. "Do I need to ask again?" he snapped. "I said no stops. Get the necklace and come straight home. What happened?"

Claber cleared his throat. "We stopped in Idaho Falls to get a bite—"

Truman held up a hand, frowning. "What were you doing in Idaho?" He knew from the news reports that the girls were from there. But that wasn't the route home. His men should never have been in that state.

"Got a call from our contact in Idaho Falls. Said he needed a new cover, that the police were suspicious. So we drove up to take care of business."

Yes, Truman conceded, such a thing could happen. "Why wasn't I notified?"

Claber lifted his chin, meeting Truman's gaze straight on. "I assumed he called you first. Idaho's not far from our Montana entry. I figured we'd kill two birds with one stone."

It wasn't what Truman would have done. But Claber had been in charge of the raid. "Go on. What did the contact say?"

"We relocated him and gave him a new cover. Since he knew we were coming, he had already bribed the mall security guard for us. It should've been quick and easy."

Already bribed the mall security? What mall security? It took Truman a half a second to put the two together. The contact arranged a get-rich-quick scheme just for Truman. But some things just didn't fit. "Where'd the girls come from?" He slammed his fist down on the desk. "I'm a jewel thief, not a kidnapper. I'm wanted for burglary, not murder!" The end of the sentence came out in a hiss, and Truman let it linger. He glowered at his man.

"They were spying on us," Claber said. His gaze wavered. "It was either kill them or bring them along. They'd seen too much."

Truman snorted. He didn't believe that for a second. "They saw a black van! You should've drugged them and dumped them in a ditch! And the girl that's dead. What happened there?"

"She was running to flag down a Jeep."

The last thing Truman needed was a murdered girl next to the Canadian border. "What, are we going to leave a trail of dead bodies from Idaho to Canada? Lead them right to us?" He pinched the bridge of his nose, some of his fury giving way to weariness. "You, of all people, know what's on my head. No false moves. We can't afford it. Everything we pull in this year goes to paying that debt, understand?" He dropped his hand and looked at Claber. "At least we've still got the Swan Lake necklace." He stared at him, waiting for confirmation. Claber bobbed his head in affirmation.

Sliding off the desk, Truman opened a drawer behind it and pulled out another whiskey bottle. The truth of the matter was, he had three girls in his house and didn't know what to do with them. Ransoms rarely worked. Police got involved, tracked them down. His whole organization would crash down like a house of cards. Not even his connections with the local force would hide him.

A dark thought twisted its way into his mind. *Girls are worth money.*

He wasn't sure where the thought came from. Only truly sick people dealt in human trafficking.

And yet, he knew it was more lucrative than weapons, than even drugs. But also one of the most risky, and Truman wanted no part of it.

Still, he knew people who trafficked. Maybe this wouldn't be such a bad move. He could get rid of the girls and cross off some of his debt at the same time.

Sid was a familiar contact, someone his father had known. He had a summer home here in Canada, but Truman didn't know where the man was right now. He would come to Montreal if he was interested. Truman could make him interested. "Claber, get me Sid. He'll buy each of those girls for half a million, maybe more. We're still in the game."

Claber stepped over to the desk and scanned a list of phone numbers taped to the inside of the drawer. "Hold on, Truman. I'll call Sid, but didn't you recognize the little Latina girl? That's Gregorio Rivera's daughter."

Truman squinted at Claber. The name didn't ring any bells.

"Who's Gregorio Rivera?"

"The *Carnicero*."

Truman jerked backward, bumping the bookcase behind him. "What? Are you sure?"

Claber nodded. "Found pictures that match the one I took in Mexico."

"Gregorio Rivera? Is that his real name?"

"It's the one he goes by in the States. I researched the girls on the drive. I found him when I got onto the girl's Facebook account. He's kept himself mostly invisible, but he forgot to think about his daughter's Facebook page. Family pictures everywhere. It's him. He's her father."

"Well." Finally, a bit of fortune. "We'll have to think about this. Assuming that man really is the *Carnicero*, and assuming he's really her father, she's worth a lot more. Quite a bit more."

"My thoughts exactly." Claber nodded.

Truman drummed his fingers on the desk. "We have to be one hundred percent sure they're who we think they are."

Claber patted the camera he kept with him. "We can send an agent to check her house. It'll be easy to find now that we know her name. We watch him for a day or two, we'll know if he does lengthy foreign travels."

"Yes." Truman gave a wry smile. "Nice of the police to give us their information. If she really is his daughter, we can demand a much higher price for her." He jerked his head at Claber. "Get someone on it."

"Yes, sir."

Truman swatted at the dusty desk and sat on it. The half-empty bottle of whiskey stood like a silent sentinel. He eyed it, tempted to take another swig. He gave in and swallowed, trying to moisten his dry throat.

Standing again, Truman paced the room. He was running out of money, and he needed more if he was to keep his finely tuned orchestra playing. He came to a decision. "Even if she's the *Carnicero*'s daughter, I don't want her. But Sid will. Make that call, Claber."

Claber pulled out his cell phone.

Stealing wasn't such a bad crime. Most of the money he made went back to the community, instead of sitting and rotting in some museum. But last week he'd added murder of a civilian to his criminal activities. This week, kidnapping.

Would he add slavery next week?

Truman stopped pacing, coming to a halt in front of Claber. He clasped his hands behind his back. "Everything we pull in right now goes to paying off McAllister."

"Truman." Claber held out his phone. "Sid."

Truman accepted it, already anticipating Sid's slimy voice that left a foul coating in his mind. "Sid. How would you like to do some business?"

CHAPTER 10

Truman hung up and handed the phone back. "Well. He's more than willing to negotiate. How much did you bring in from the raid?"

Claber's shoulders relaxed, and he seated himself in the chair in front of the desk. He obviously thought he was out of the fire. "The necklace is worth two million. We only got a handful at the jewelry store before the girls created a distraction, but I think we pulled a quarter of a million there."

"It's in the safe?"

"As soon as we got here."

Truman nodded. "Good." He paused, letting his thoughts wander. "I have no idea how much I'll be able to get for the girls. I've never done anything like this." There were lines he'd told himself he'd never cross, yet here he was. "I want a million for each. Three million total."

"That's a bit high, Boss. Even the best markets usually only pay half a million for each girl."

That hardly seemed worth it. He could make that much in a few jewelry raids. But Sid rolled in the dough, with vacation homes across the world. How did he find his girls, and where did he sell them? Truman didn't want to know. "But one is the *Carnicero's* daughter, right? Two million for the three girls."

Claber leaned forward. "And where are we getting the other

millions?"

Truman stiffened his jaw to keep from grimacing. If he had a year, he could bring that money in, easy. But a month? Less? He wasn't sure it was possible. "I don't know. McAllister's getting impatient. I'm not sure he'll give me the full time to find it."

"And if he doesn't?" Claber asked softly.

"I'm planning an escape route. If we leave here, we split up. You'll take a contingency and I'll take one. We'll liquidate everything we have as quickly as possible, then rendezvous somewhere far away." *Somewhere unreachable.* "I'll give you the full details when I have them."

Claber leaned back, his green eyes thoughtful. "We could kidnap more girls. It wasn't hard."

Truman stood up, angered by Claber's crassness. "No. That's not what I do." *I'm not one of them.* "We're doing four raids this week. Get teams of three men each together. I want the raids done at the same time. No time for the stores to tip each other off."

"Where?"

"Stay away from Texas and Idaho. Do the Midwest. It's been awhile."

"Kentucky it is." Claber lifted out of his chair. "Did you want me to find a way to contact the *Carnicero*?"

"Yes. Lure him out of hiding. In fact." Truman tapped his chin. Did he dare dangle a ransom in front of the *Carnicero*? This man was notorious for finding and annihilating the most secretive of operations. A ransom might simply make Truman a bigger target.

Or it might get him the money he needed. "Let's wait to see what Sid offers me. And then we'll triple it and ask for it as ransom. No, quadruple it. If the *Carnicero* wants his daughter, he'll pay for her."

"Assuming he wants her."

"Yes." Truman narrowed his eyes. "Assuming."

Truman opened his tablet, updating his file sheets with information about the raids and the money they'd brought in. This was a business, after all, and he kept organized records.

The girls must still be cleaning. He hadn't seen them since the night before, and he'd given Claber orders to manage them all day. But it was time to meet with them. He owed them an explanation.

He stepped out of his office and hesitated. What role should he take with them? The kind, sympathetic, accidental kidnapper? Or the harsh "tough-luck" kind of guy?

He wandered into the game room, where several men spread out on couches, sleeping. He had to expect that, since he kept them up in the night traveling or planning raids.

"Grey." Truman tapped Grey's foot with his own, waking the man.

"Hmm?" Grey sat up, rubbing his pale eyes. "Boss. What is it?"

"I need you to prepare a formal dinner for tonight."

Grey blinked several times, stretching his arms behind his shoulders. "Okay. How many guests?"

"Four." Truman paused, then said, "The girls you kidnapped, and me."

That got Grey's attention. He dropped his arms, jaw gaping open. "You're going to eat dinner with them?"

Truman held his gaze, keeping his eyes stern. "Yes. And a nice one."

Grey inhaled and shoved his fingers though his wavy brown hair. "I'm not trying to say you shouldn't. But it might be a better idea to keep distance between you."

Truman considered that. He did feel a need to establish a hierarchy; the girls had to know he was in charge. But he didn't want to make this any more miserable for them than it was. "I have to explain things to them. And I have questions for them."

"But you can't be on equal footing."

Truman crossed his arms over his chest. "What do you suggest?"

"Meet with them, if you want." Grey nodded. "Yes, that's fine. Eat dinner with them, even. But don't serve them what you eat. Make them see that they're subservient."

Subservient. An ugly word.

"Boss," Grey said, and Truman heard the sincerity in his tone, "I know this isn't your thing. Look, it's not mine. We had to save our backs, though. At least we didn't kill them all."

"At least," Truman grunted.

"You can't let them think you're soft. They'll take advantage of you."

Grey was right. Truman hated to admit it. He had to maintain order. The consequences for their actions had to be severe. "Fine. Prepare the dining room. Make them something simple, soup and bread, whatever."

A glint came into Grey's eye. "And something nice for you."

"Yes."

Grey got to his feet, brushing his pants, his hands twitching with excitement. Truman would never understand Grey's love for the kitchen. "I'll take the Camaro to the store, then?"

"Go." Truman waved him away.

Grey was right. What was he thinking? He couldn't very well strike up a friendship with the girls and then sell them into slavery.

He stopped at the mirror in the entryway and examined his reflection. Shadows hung under his eyes, a dark contrast to the gauntness of his pale face. He didn't like what he saw.

———

Everything about the mansion Truman's father had left him was ornate. From the red carpet in the entryway to the marble busts on the show room, it had the detail and expense of a museum.

The dining room was no exception. Truman didn't entertain often because he kept his location a secret. But a long wood table took up the middle of the room for the occasions when he needed it. White pillars took away the sharp edges of the corners, and crown molding ran along the top of the tiered ceiling. Murals of fruits in pastels covered one entire wall.

Truman trailed his fingers down the white tablecloth, admiring Grey's handy work. That man had missed his calling in life. Here he led the life of crime when he could be gainfully and happily employed as a chef somewhere. Platters of gourmet foods covered the table, from cuts of beef with gravy to honey-glazed vegetables. Truman shook his head. He couldn't eat all this. It was more "in your face" than "I'm in charge."

Three other chairs had been placed around the table. In front of each chair sat a bowl with green soup in it. Truman resisted the childish urge to wrinkle his nose. Green soup?

"Grey," he called, and Grey's footsteps echoed along the tiled flooring before he emerged from a servant's door.

Dressed in jeans and a long-sleeved t-shirt, Grey looked like a construction worker, not a chef. "Yes?"

"This is too much." Truman gestured at the food.

Grey bobbed his head. "I'm sure the guys will eat the leftovers."

The message was clear: This is not for the girls. "Find Claber," Truman said. "Tell him to bring the girls in."

"You got it."

Truman tapped his fork on the cloth. He heard Claber approach and stood up again. Pressing his hands down the front of his shirt, he smoothed out any last wrinkles, then berated himself for worrying about such a thing.

One of the heavy French doors opened, and the three girls shuffled in. They stared at the ground and came to a stop just inside the dining room. The tallest of the girls, the one with red hair, kept lifting her eyes and darting them back down.

Amanda Murphy, Truman reminded himself. Their names should not be important to him. And yet, they were.

Interesting how she wasn't frightened. Or at least, she was more curious than frightened. He filed that information away under her name.

Now what? Truman stared at them. How did a kidnapper act? He inclined his head, catching himself before he extended a complete bow. They would see that as a mocking gesture. "Please, sit." He motioned to the chairs around the table.

The brunette—the *Carnicero*'s daughter, if Claber had his facts straight—lifted her face, gaze flicking over the table. Jacinta Rivera. Truman searched her face, looking for a resemblance to the vigilante. He knew from the way her nostrils flared that she was hungry. They all had to be.

They ambled forward, slowly, as if expecting him to spring a trap. When nothing happened, they sat down around the table, still silent, still glancing around in suspicion.

Could he blame them?

He had a show to put on. Truman began piling his plate high with food from different dishes. He glanced at the girls as he speared a long piece of broccoli. Their eyes were on him. More precisely, on his food. None of them had touched their soup.

He suppressed a sigh. So much food here. Plenty for them to have some. *Don't*, he told himself. "I don't particularly like the color of pea soup either." He spotted a cloth-covered basket in the middle of the table, within reach of the girls. He doubted Grey baked his fresh rolls anticipating that the kidnapped girls would eat them, but Truman couldn't deny them that much. Besides, bread and soup went together. "There's fresh bread." He pointed his fork at the basket.

That got their attention. All three began sticking their hands in for rolls. Rivera grabbed a handful and dumped them in her lap. Truman watched her take a bite and close her eyes. Maybe Grey was wrong. Maybe he could accomplish more with them if they didn't feel intimidated by him.

She opened her eyes and they met his. She ducked her head, splotchy redness creeping up her face. Grabbing her spoon, she poked at her soup.

No. It was too late. No matter what he did, they would never trust him. "So." He placed some golden, deep-fried shrimp on his plate, despite the fact that he had no appetite. "Why were you watching the robbery?"

No one answered. He looked at Murphy, the redhead, who sat on his left. "Well?"

She didn't look at him, and his eyes fell on Sara Yadle, the youngest of the group. That shiver of delight and surprise ran through him again.

Becca. Except she wasn't Becca. He had to keep reminding himself of that. Yet the feeling of familiarity wouldn't fade. He couldn't make himself not care for her. Putting a gruff note in his voice, he said, "What do you think, girl?"

Sara's eyes lifted from her bowl. "Curiosity."

He raised an eyebrow. Was she the only one brave enough to respond to him? "Dangerous." Not a surprise, though. Many of the troublesome endeavors he participated in as a child began with curiosity.

He examined them while they sipped their soups and tried to

see them as objects, expensive items for him to do what he pleased with. "Such beautiful girls." None of them responded, except to maybe huddle down further in their chairs.

While he knew he should maintain the distance between them, a part of him wanted to draw them out of their shells. He didn't have guests often, and he was curious about them. "Do you have names? How about it? Red?" He nodded at Murphy. "By far the most beautiful in the group. Exquisite beauty." His eyes were drawn to Sara, again against his will. "And you are nothing but a child. Yet your innocence is so—captivating." He frowned, stopping his words. *Careful, Truman.* He couldn't feed this fascination with her. He forced himself to turn to Rivera. Their salvation. He could see some of the features from the man in the photograph, now that he looked. She was his daughter. She had to be. Now he just needed to make sure it really was the *Carnicero*. "And you."

She met his eyes. "What about you? We don't know your name."

"Of course you do. Who else would I be, but The Hand?"

The girl exchanged a glance with the redhead, then looked away.

Truman cleared his throat. They should know he had connections everywhere. "Never mind. I already know who you are. You're all over the news, though the police are hesitant to link your disappearance to the robbery."

The police had saved him more often than they knew, and he meant the real ones, not the planted agents who worked to keep his name off the radar.

Someone would connect the dots, though. Some ambitious policeman or detective would come along, say to hell with conventions, and put two and two together. "They haven't found your friend's body yet. That will throw them off track; I don't usually deal in homicides." He said the words lightly, as if her death were no

69

big deal. But he felt it, like another rock added to the sack of burdens he carried.

The *Carnicero*'s daughter choked, a soft sound that could have been a sob. She reached for her cup of water and knocked it over.

Truman clenched his fists. *I'm sorry. It never should have happened.* He couldn't say that. Not exactly.

Grey was right. He was too soft, and they would prey on him. "An unfortunate incident. I do regret it." He began to cut his steak, keeping his eyes on his plate now. "Life is cruel. There's no way around it." Damn this whole situation. They shouldn't be here. Yet here they were.

He shoved some of the cut steak into their bowls as if he were feeding Barley. "Eat. I'm not trying to starve you. You're no good to me dead." They fished around in the green muck for the meat he'd left them. They weren't starving yet, but watching them devour the tiny pieces of steak was pathetic. He stood up, pushing his chair away from the table. "Grey."

Grey entered quickly, as if he'd been waiting just outside the room.

"I'm done. Get them back to the attic." Truman strode out of the room, trying to escape the acrid taste in his mouth.

CHAPTER 11

He went straight to his office. His head pounded with too many thoughts. He shouldn't have eaten with them. He didn't want to know them. He didn't need to know who they were. Suddenly they seemed more real to him, and he resented it.

Out. They had to get out of his house.

Truman settled himself behind the desk, sinking into the padded chair. Where was Barley when he needed him? Sid should be in Canada by now. Truman scrolled through his contacts and pressed send.

"Hello," Sid greeted, his voice smooth and mirthful all at the same time.

How did Sid manage that? He didn't know who was calling. He had no fear, no concern for those who might wish to end his career. "It's Truman."

"Truman." The smile came through the phone. "What can I do for you?"

Truman gritted his teeth, wanting to wash his phone of Sid's sliminess. "Are you in Canada yet?"

"Yes, arrived just yesterday. You ready to enact our deal?"

"I'm ready to discuss things, yes." Truman led out a careful breath, hoping Sid didn't notice his anxiety. He needed to get these girls out of his house. "I'd like to meet with you tomorrow."

"Certainly. I'm free in the morning. You remember where the house is?"

"I can find it again." Truman had only been to Sid's Montreal residence one time, right after he inherited his father's accounts. Sid had insisted on offering his help to Truman as he established himself.

Truman had rejected his help, and managed to make a name for himself without it. But the fact that the man had built a replica of a South American summer home, complete with palm trees, in the northern part of North America, said a lot about what he expected reality to do for him: Bend.

"Good," Sid replied. "We'll see you at ten. I'll have breakfast ready."

Truman hung up and drummed his fingers on the desk. Within a week, the girls would be gone, and Truman would have a little bit of extra money, as well. Just a little bit. It made him nervous to leave the girls at the house without him, though.

He opened the desk drawer and scanned the list of phone numbers. Fayande was their contact inside the Montreal police force, and his number topped the list. Truman dialed the number.

French words carried through the receiver, and Truman cut him off with, "Officer Fayande?"

The French stopped, and the man said in crisp English, "Yes. Who is calling?"

"The Canadian White House," Truman said, spouting out their code words.

Fayande didn't miss a beat, but Truman knew he was paying attention now. The tips Truman paid him more than doubled his police salary. "How can I assist?"

"I need two or three of your men to pay me a visit tomorrow morning, about nine a.m. Can that be arranged?"

"I believe so," Fayande said, his voice cordial and unassuming.

"Make sure you know their loyalties." The police would see the kidnapped girls, and he couldn't risk an officer he didn't know trying to be a hero.

"I will make sure."

"That's all, then." Truman hung up the phone, feeling reassured. With the police nearby, there would be an added level of security for the girls.

He switched on his tablet and opened his online bank account. Finding Fayande's account, he transferred over several thousand. It was the only way to guarantee his silence.

Truman retired to his room early. He'd spent some time in the game room, but the men were skittish. All conversation stopped when he came in, and over card games and movies they shot him surreptitious glances.

Because of the girls. They didn't belong here, and all the men were high-strung, Truman included. He knew Claber had taken charge of them again, finding some project or task that needed to be done around the house.

Truman stayed out of his way. He avoided running into the girls, especially after the disastrous dinner the night before. He cursed himself for meddling. Now they weren't faceless names to him. They were scared girls.

He loaded a movie on his phone, but it didn't hold his interest. Becca. Thoughts of the beautiful blond entered his mind. She'd plagued him ever since he'd seen Sara. He combed his fingers through his hair, remembering the way Becca's long nails would scrape over his scalp as she played with his hair.

Rising from the bed, he crossed to the balcony and stared out over the descending trees. What if Becca hadn't died? Where would their love be now?

Becca's image merged with Sara's, the kidnapped girl. He knew she wasn't Becca, but at the same time his heart latched on to her, placing all his emotional attachment to Becca on her.

Second chance.

The words whispered past his hair, tickling his face as they carried on the breeze. The wind didn't give advice, but Truman's heart beat in time to the words. Second chance.

Was it possible? He had to talk to her. He'd never know otherwise. He returned to the nightstand and used his phone to call Claber.

"Yes?" Claber answered. He probably suspected it was Truman, but since the number showed up as restricted, he couldn't know for sure.

"Where are the girls?"

"They're washing the dishes and cleaning the kitchen. They should be done soon."

At least his house was getting cleaner. "I want to speak to the blond girl. Sara. Bring her to me." Truman kept his voice professional, cold. He couldn't give away his emotional link to this girl.

"Now?"

"No." The other girls would notice if Sara disappeared right now, and they would likely mutiny. Victims went along almost willingly until they felt threatened. He had to keep them feeling secure. "When you take them to bed. Send the other two up the ladder first, then close the hatch before she follows."

"Got it," Claber said. There was no confusion in his voice, no uncertainty about his orders.

Truman relaxed and hung up the phone. The decision had been made. He would meet her and see what she thought of him.

She arrived twenty minutes later. Claber knocked, and Truman, still dressed in his khaki pants and plaid button-up shirt, opened the door. His heart skipped a beat when he saw her, the long blond hair falling over her face as she stared at her feet. She was really here.

Truman met Claber's eyes and gave a short nod, then pulled her into the room. He closed the door, not bothering to lock it. She wouldn't run. She could if she wanted to; he wouldn't force to her stay.

She didn't lift her head, and it was so easy to believe she was Becca. Except Becca would say something. She'd toss her hair, show the dimple in her left cheek as she smiled, her eyes crinkling in happiness.

"I'm not going to hurt you." Truman unfolded a chair by the nightstand and sat, eager to show her his intentions. "I just want to talk to you."

Still she said nothing, and he began to get the uneasy feeling that this was a bad idea. What did he plan on saying, anyway? Sorry for kidnapping you? "Do you go by Sara?"

Silence. He shifted, sweat prickling his hairline. He felt as uncertain and nervous as a grade-schooler. "Would you like anything? Something to eat?" Images of their pea soup dinner flickered through his mind, and he winced. "You don't have to stand there. Sit."

She didn't move. Maybe she didn't know where to sit. True, he had the only chair. Truman exhaled, realizing he'd just have to show her. He stood up and took her hand. Sara flinched and yanked it back, tucking her fists into her side.

His hand ached where he'd touched her skin. He softened his voice. "I won't hurt you. Come on." Taking her forearm in a gentle grip, he guided her to the bed. She didn't fight him, but seemed to take longer to lift her feet with every step. In the end Truman plucked her up and sat her down in the middle of the bed, a little impatient with her fear of him. Then he settled himself down in his chair, several feet away.

"There. I'm not even close to you. I want to help you, Sara."

She clasped her hands in front of her, not meeting his eyes.

Like a little girl. She looked so vulnerable, so scared. He knew in that moment that he couldn't sell her to Sid. He couldn't bear for someone to take her, to possess her, to strip her of her innocence.

But how? How could he keep her from Sid?

He could claim her as his.

The idea lighted in his thoughts, and the room seemed to brighten. He never wanted to be in this world of crime. Here was his chance to pursue a different endeavor.

He got up from the chair and sat cross-legged in front of her on the bed. He tucked a strand of hair behind her ear, trying to see her face. Not Becca. Sara. He lifted her chin, but she met his eyes only briefly before closing them. Her lips moved but no sound came out, and then a tear rolled down one cheek, followed by another on the other side. She squeezed her eyes shut and turned her head, pulling her arms close to her body as if to shut him out.

Her obvious despair tugged at his heart. Truman moved closer and put his hand behind her head. She froze, even the sniffles stopping. With a sigh, he removed his hand. "Sara, don't be afraid of me. I'll do anything for you. You're safe now. You can have anything you want, anything at all."

Even as the words left his mouth, it dawned on him what he was offering her. More than just freedom. He was offering her the chance to be his equal, to be a part of his empire.

He reached over and clasped her hand, but she tightened her fingers into a fist. She whispered something, a tear trailing down her face and dripping from her chin.

"What?" Truman leaned in closer.

"Take me back."

"Back where?" he asked, before comprehension hit him. Hit him hard, like an iron fist to the gut. "Back to the attic?" But certainly she'd rather be with him than in there. Here she had everything. There she was a prisoner.

She only nodded, the tears chasing each other down her cheeks.

He stared at her, a rock in his chest. All his attempts to make her feel safe had failed. She didn't want to be with him. Well, he certainly hoped she adjusted, because he wasn't selling her to Sid. He'd give her some space, wait for her to come around.

Truman picked up his phone and called Claber. His eyes never left Sara as he said, "Come get the girl. You can take her back now."

CHAPTER 12

Truman awoke with his stomach churning. In an instant, his failed visit with Sara came back to him, and he grimaced. Somehow he had to gain her trust. Make her not fear him.

But right now he couldn't worry about her. He needed to clear his emotions and focus on his upcoming meeting with Sid. He selected his wardrobe carefully, wanting to look casual but important, like money was no issue. Khaki pants and a leather jacket.

He opened his bedroom door and nearly tripped over Barley. "Hey boy," he said, bending to scratch behind his ears. Barley whined in appreciation, pushing his head into Truman's hand.

"I haven't seen much of you since the girls got here." Truman rubbed Barley's golden fur a bit longer as he considered Sara. He looked back at the dog and gave him a pat on his side. Truman ushered Barley into his room, shutting him inside. He'd follow the girls around if left out.

Truman bumped into Sanders on the second landing. "Sanders. You help Claber with those girls today. I'm taking them to a buyer tonight, so I want them all cleaned up."

Sanders nodded, the spike in his blond hair jiggling. "Got it."

"Oh, and the police will be here in about an hour. They'll make sure nothing goes wrong while I'm gone," Truman said. He continued on out to the garage, where Claber and Eli prepped the bright yellow Camaro. Eli filled the car with gas from a portable tank kept in the garage.

"Why don't you just take the girls to Sid now? Get rid of them," Claber murmured close to his ear.

"I want to hear his price first. I can't gamble effectively with them hanging off me."

Claber arched a brow. "How long will this take?"

Truman shrugged. "If he's agreeable, I hope to sign tonight. Unless something comes through with the *Carnicero*."

Claber shifted his weight. "Should we hang on to her longer, just in case?"

Truman shook his head. "No. We'll just sell her for a higher price to Sid. Then he can deal with the *Carnicero* directly."

Claber nodded. Truman watched his second-in-command. Tonight might not be soon enough. He would breathe a deep sigh of relief when those girls were gone.

Eli put down the gas tank, his fat lower lip poofing out. "Car's ready."

"Let's go, then." Truman gestured for him to get in the driver's side. "I'll direct you to Sid's place."

A motion in his peripheral vision caught his eye. Truman cocked his head and saw Rivera and Murphy peering at him through the small round window in the attic.

Enjoy your little room, Truman thought. *Soon you'll be elsewhere.* He didn't try to imagine where "elsewhere" was. He wanted them off his hands. If that meant his hands got a little muddy in the process, so be it.

The engine roared, and Truman climbed in, feeding Eli directions. He lowered the window, feeling the nippy autumn air pull into the car. He watched the tall oak trees fly past and felt the exhilarating freedom that came with taking charge of life. Even the circumstances surrounding the sale couldn't change the fact that Truman would lighten his debt with this. Ridding himself of the girls bought a little more breathing room, and so they had to go.

Except Sara.

Sara. He blinked, taken back by how much emotion the name carried with it. She was worth more than money. He'd make her forget the past, and she'd be happy.

The drive to Sid's house took a little over an hour. The September sun shone on the red brick driveway, reflecting off the large glass windows surrounding the house. Truman pulled out his sunglasses.

"I'll have my phone on me," he said to Eli, "but don't you dare interrupt us. Not unless it's an emergency."

"Yes, sir."

A servant opened the car door for Truman, and he stepped out. Large palm trees waved in the wind. Truman resisted the urge to roll his eyes. Palm trees. In Canada. Tall lamps blended into the foliage above them, giving them the additional heat and light they needed to live in this climate.

Money to burn. He made a mental note to raise the price of the girls. "Wait here," he said to Eli.

Sid strode to the car, looking comfortable in Bermuda shorts and flip-flops, and greeted him with a large smile.

Truman forced his lips to curl upward. "Sid."

"Never thought I'd be doing business with you," the other man laughed. The gel in his wavy brown hair glistened in the sunlight.

His laugh made Truman's skin crawl. His gut twisted, and he wondered if this was such a good idea. Was it too late? Could he just let the girls go?

No. McAllister had that debt over his head, and he'd hunt Truman down. "The development was definitely unexpected. But I'm sure it will be beneficial for us both." He glanced at Eli, who nodded at him from the driver's seat. Truman returned the nod before giving all his attention to Sid.

"Shall we?" The other man grinned and extended a hand down the tiled walkway.

Truman followed Sid through the immaculate lawn into the front sunroom. The warmth coming through the glass and the tiled walls made Truman feel like he really was in South America.

"You've got three little ladies, you say?" Sid asked, stopping at an entry room table and opening a drawer.

Truman's jaw tensed, and he cleared his throat. "Just two."

Sid raised an eyebrow. "Oh? I was certain you'd said three." He placed a silver platter on the table.

"I'm keeping one," Truman said, irritated that he had to say even that much. Sid didn't deserve an explanation.

"Ah." Sid leered. "Never knew what you were missing, huh?" He handed the silver platter to his servant.

This time Truman didn't bother with a response, though his blood boiled at the crass reference.

Sid shrugged, then motioned him into one of his wicker chairs while he sank back into a large black leather couch.

Truman removed his outer jacket and placed it on the table, then sat in the chair.

"Cigar?" Sid offered as the servant returned. Now several cigars decorated the ornate platter.

"Thank you." Truman accepted one and let the servant light it. He inhaled, allowing it to calm his nerves. *Let's get this over with.*

His phone began to jingle, and he pulled it out. Eli. Truman's brows knit together and a knot formed in his stomach. He had specifically said not to interrupt him. Why would Eli call him now? He looked at Sid. "May I?"

"Of course."

He answered the call. "What?" He hoped his irritation showed through. *This better be important.*

"I just got a call from Sanders. There's been a problem." Eli's voice came across restrained, with a current of urgent energy beneath it.

That bad feeling in his gut intensified. "A problem with what?" he hissed. Out of his peripheral vision, he saw Sid lean forward. Truman forced his body to relax.

Eli's brief hesitation said enough, and Truman interrupted himself. "Never mind. I'll call Claber myself." He disconnected, then stood up. "Excuse me."

Leaving the sunroom, Truman settled himself into a corner of the foyer. Claber answered on the first ring.

"Claber. What happened?"

Instead of Claber, it was Sanders' excited voice that shouted in his ear, and Truman winced. "The girls escaped! They're not in the house!"

Truman stiffened. "What?" He'd expected bad news, but this wasn't possible. "They're gone?" No, no, no. This couldn't be happening. "All of them?" Not Sara. Perhaps she hadn't been with the others...

"Yes, yes," Sanders said. "All of them."

Truman's mind flashed back to the officers he'd requested to come out to the house. "What about the police? Where are they?"

"They searched too! We couldn't find the girls and they finally had to leave. The cops said they'd tell the situation to Fayande. The girls ran out into the forest. Claber's there now. He left his phone with me."

"Why didn't someone contact me sooner?" Truman snarled.

Silence was the only answer, but Truman already knew why. Of course his men had hoped to find the girls before any harm was done. Now when it was apparent that the girls were gone, they were forced to tell him.

His head ached. The web entangling him tightened, strangling the breath out of him. "Keep looking. Send a car to patrol the road beneath the mountain. They have to emerge somewhere." He glanced toward the sunroom and saw Sid leaning back in his seat, touching his fingertips together. "I'll call again when I leave here."

Truman flashed Sid a grimace and returned to his chair, eyeing his abandoned cigar as it smoked in the ashtray on the coffee table.

"Well?" Sid asked in an irritatingly mellow voice.

Truman gathered his jacket. "I'm afraid we'll have to continue these arrangements later. Thank you for your time."

Sid chuckled as Truman hurried to the door. "Anytime, my man. Anytime."

Truman didn't respond. Sid's patronizing tone made the blood rush through his veins. He had to get those girls.

CHAPTER 13

The drive back lasted an eternity. He didn't wait for Eli to put the vehicle in park before he jumped out of the passenger side. He headed toward the front door, where Claber greeted him.

"Well?" Truman clenched his hands. "Did you find them?"

Claber shook his head, his eyes staring at some spot over Truman's head. "We know they escaped into the forest, but I didn't see any sign of them. We've posted men at different positions along the road; we'll find them when they come out."

"You better," Truman snapped, rabid anger firing through his veins. "Their lives are worth more than yours." Everything was gone. Everything. A momentary wave of grief washed over him, so fierce that Truman dug his fingernails into his hands. Where was Sara now? He had to find her.

Then a sea of rage burned away his sadness. The other two girls had taken his freedom with them. At least he still had the necklace and the jewels.

He hadn't even seen the necklace yet. He'd been so caught up with the girls after the raid party returned, he'd forgotten to ask to see it. Now a safety net of diamonds would give him a little reassurance. "Where's the Swan Lake necklace? Is it in the safe?"

Claber paused just a moment too long, letting Truman know that he hadn't given the necklace much thought after the kidnapping either. "I don't know. Would you like me to check?"

That response didn't sit well with him. "I'll do it myself," Truman grunted, pushing past him.

The safe was hidden in a small utility closet on the second floor. Unlatching the back wall, Truman let himself into a large room, of which the safe took up most of the space. He rubbed his fingers over his palms, noting how clammy they were. Something didn't feel right. *It's in the safe*, he told himself, unable to calm his rapidly beating heart. He grabbed the combination lock and spun it around.

The door unhitched with a click. For once the sight of various boxes and stolen goods only infuriated him. How was he supposed to find anything in this mess? He yanked everything out, dumping the contents on the floor, certain at any second he'd find that necklace.

He didn't. A little more desperate this time, he carefully put everything back in place, searching every box and corner.

Nothing. He stood up and stared at the contents of the safe.

Claber remained in the hallway, a silent observer, his brows knit together. "Is it there?"

A current of unease ran through Claber's voice. Claber knew, as Truman did, that without the girls and the necklace, they had nothing to stand on. The money would not come in fast enough and they would have wasted the last two weeks. Half their time. There would be no hope.

"No." Truman bit out the word, pouring his rage into the single syllable. His hands trembled with fury, and he took several deep breaths. The room spun for a moment. Spinning out of control.

"We'll check the van," Claber said, a bead of sweat forming along his buzzed hairline. "Maybe it never got moved."

Truman didn't answer. He strode down the hall, letting the safe swing shut behind him. Claber marched to keep up.

The van was safely locked in the garage. At least one thing was where it should be.

"There's nothing in the back," Claber said, doing a quick scan before closing the doors to the cargo hold. "Everything in here was put in the safe."

Truman yanked the passenger side door open and bent to pull out the safety deposit box under the seat. It wasn't even sealed. He opened it, already knowing it would be empty. Swearing viciously, he shoved the box back under the seat and began opening glove compartments, checking cup holders. Claber hovered behind him like a nervous phantom.

"Check the driver's side!" Truman yelled.

Claber did so. He looked a little white as they concluded their search. "It's not here."

Truman paused, breathing heavily, leaning on the open passenger door. He realized from the cold pit in his stomach that he had been expecting that answer. He inhaled as two pieces suddenly clicked together. "The girls were in the cargo hold."

"Yes, that's where we put them."

"That's where you put the stolen jewels, also."

Claber swallowed and swung his eyes around as if he desired to be anywhere but there. "Yes, sir."

Truman slammed the door shut, his eyes burning. He swatted at them and unclenched his jaw. "Get the men into my office. Tell them the situation."

He ran up the steps to the house, not waiting for Claber's answer. The necklace and the girls were gone, and somebody was going to pay.

He stopped at the kitchen long enough to open a flask of whiskey and take a swig. Hopefully that gave Claber enough time to gather everyone; he wanted them waiting in his office when he got there.

They were perched around the room when he entered, all who weren't on a raid or being held hostage. He scanned them before he entered, noting the way some hunched over as if to appear smaller, and others stood straight with their shoulders back, ready to take it on. He pushed down the feelings of loyalty and camaraderie that he felt for each of them. Somewhere, respect had been replaced by casualness, and now discipline must replace friendship if he were to come out of this alive.

"Who's responsible for this stupidity?" Truman roared, entering the room and unholstering his pistol. He waved it around, eyes landing on the three who had led the raid: Eli, Grey, and Claber. "Why wasn't the necklace in the safe where it should've been?"

Eli gulped, and then stepped forward. "I placed the box in the back of the van with the other stolen goods. I didn't think to move it after we picked up the girls. It happened quickly and I was—a little tired." He waved one hand in a futile dismissal of his actions, his fat lower lip wobbling.

Truman marched forward so quickly that the man was forced to step backwards, rejoining his comrades in line. "Because of that one small mistake, the necklace was in the back with the girls. The girls! And they're gone! And so is the necklace!" Before he could change his mind, Truman aimed the gun at Eli and pulled the trigger. He liked Eli, and he knew he'd regret killing him later.

But he couldn't think of that now. Chaos had taken over, and he needed order. A little fear could work wonders. They'd lost fear and respect. He was going to help them get it back. If the death of one man could do that, it would be a purpose well-served.

The other men averted their eyes from Eli's fallen body. Truman had their undivided attention. He lowered his voice. "He wasn't the only one at fault. Who was supposed to make sure the necklace made it safely into the vault?"

With an audible sigh, Grey stepped forward. "That was me, sir," he admitted, his expression flat, his face slightly paler than usual. "I brought in all the boxes that were in the hold and put them in the vault.

But I didn't open them and check."

Truman stepped up to him, his nose inches from Grey's cheek, but Grey didn't move. He kept his face forward, unblinking. "I'm not going to kill you. But I will if we don't get that necklace back. Understood?"

The lines around Grey's eyes relaxed, and he nodded. "Yes, sir. I'll recover those girls."

"I know." Truman stepped back again. Once more his eyes swept over the men before him. "None of us will get any pay if the necklace and the girls are not recovered. Find them. Now!" His men filed out of the room, gingerly stepping around their fallen friend. Truman went behind his desk and sank into the chair, dropping his head into his hands. Weariness and despair flooded him like liquid lead.

The stress was getting to him. He could feel his scruples fading behind necessity. *The bright day is done, And we are for the dark.* Was he really no better than all the other criminals out there? "Claber!"

He appeared in the empty doorway. "Yes?"

"The blond girl. Sara." He struggled with the words, but there was no delicate way to say this. "I need her back here." He couldn't bear her loss. His chest ached, suffocating him, just like after Becca's accident. He wouldn't lose them both.

Claber jerked his head upward. "We'll get her back."

"That's all, then," Truman murmured, exhaling. He opened a drawer and felt around for his flask of alcohol, only to come up empty. Of course. "And bring me my whiskey."

CHAPTER 14

Truman swatted at the wet nose nudging him. Barley had been whining in his room when he'd returned there last night. The gunshots had sent a healthy amount of fear and activity into the dog as well as his men.

Barley's soft whine repeated, punctuated by a tapping sound. He groaned and rolled over. Someone was knocking on the bedroom door.

It took Truman half a minute to realize he'd fallen asleep fully dressed, sprawled across the foot of the bed. He swore and pushed himself off, stumbling toward the door and tripping over Barley on the way. He had meant to stay awake all night, waiting for news to come in from the search parties.

He unlocked the door and threw it open. Claber stood there, dark rings under his tired eyes, phone extended.

Truman glanced at his watch. Just after four in the morning. He took the phone from Claber and mouthed, "Who?"

Claber inclined his head at the device. Truman glanced down and scowled at the name glowing in the display.

He lifted the receiver and growled, "McAllister. It's four in the morning."

"Oh, right you are," McAllister said, his voice the proper mix of cheer and chagrin. "Good morning, then. How are you this fine day?"

Truman's thoughts raced. Did he know the girls were missing? Had Sid told him something? No, it couldn't be. "Fine. Things are fine."

"I'm so glad to hear it," McAllister purred. "Your days are counting down, right? How many are left?"

Truman gritted his teeth. He didn't want to have this conversation right now. "I don't have time for this, McAllister. You'll get your money."

"Well, if you need any assistance, I have a contact in Montreal. I could lend him to you. But you're not in Montreal, are you? Isn't it... Victoriaville?"

Truman couldn't stop the goosebumps of terror that popped out over his arms. He shuddered, glad McAllister couldn't see him. It was no secret that Truman lived in Canada. Anyone could guess the city was in Quebec. But knowing he lived in tiny Victoriaville wasn't a guess. McAllister was honing in on his location. How much did he know? How was he getting his information?

McAllister kept talking. "Maybe you and my contact could meet up. For some face-to-face encouragement."

"No, it won't be necessary." Truman forced the words out between clenched teeth. "Everything is under control." He disconnected the call and threw the phone on the floor. Adrenaline coursed through his veins.

He couldn't go back to sleep. He needed to prep the evacuation route from the house. Any day now, they might need it.

He went up to his office on the fourth floor and opened the desk drawer, searching for a notepad. Finding one, he began jotting down a few quick sentences. "Wanted for theft. Three housemaids." He quickly made up some information about the girls and added a large, fictitious reward.

He needed some photos. Claber probably had some on that small camera he carried everywhere. He'd send Claber to the twenty-four hour drugstore for some pictures, and then run a flyer in tomorrow's edition of the Toronto Star.

He'd have to pull some strings to get it run with tomorrow's paper, but those would probably be the easiest strings he'd have to pull for awhile.

The sun rose and still Truman hadn't slept. His phone buzzed on the table next to him, and he gave it a cursory glance before answering. Claber. "Tell me you've got good news."

"Yes," he answered, triumph in his voice. "We found the girls."

Truman straightened, relief flooding through him and making his insides weak. "Finally. Are they with you? Tie them up and gag them." No more Mr. Nice Guy. That had been a big mistake.

"No, I didn't capture them." Claber kept right on talking before Truman could express his displeasure. "They escaped in a car with a Canadian girl. But I got a picture of the car's license plate. We can track her residence. We've got them now."

Yes, that was something. "Good work. Call Fayande and give him that information. Copy me in on it. Did you get that flyer printed?"

"I did."

"What happens if someone sees the girls?"

"I saw an ad in the paper. Some college kid offering to be a research assistant. I called him, told him I'd pay him big bucks. All he has to do is answer his phone and take messages. I call him every half hour to get the messages."

Truman grunted. "Make it every fifteen minutes. And make sure you block your number when you call. How much you paying him?"

"Ten bucks every call he takes."

Fair enough. "I assume someone is going to the address right now?"

"I sent Sanders and Grey. They're posing as RCMP."

"Excellent." Truman stared at the door to his study. The barren walls mocked him. Nothing to show for his life except a twelve-year-old labrador.

He needed to start planning his next raid. But he couldn't focus. He had to find Sara. That necklace. The *Carnicero's* daughter.

His phone rang and he snatched it up before it finished. "Yes?"

"Truman? It's Grey."

"Did you find the residence?"

"Yes. The vehicle belongs to Christophe Coton. We found him at home, just returning from work."

Truman glanced at his desk clock. Ten forty-five a.m. blinked at him in digital lines. Christophe must work at night. "And the car? The girls? Were they there?"

"No, sir. He lent the car to his girlfriend, Natalie. We got her address. He also had her cell phone." A smug note entered Grey's voice. "We tapped it."

"Of course." Truman didn't congratulate him. "Are you on your way to Natalie's house?"

"Yes. We will be there in twenty minutes."

"If she's not there, find out where she took those girls."

"Hopefully to the police," Grey said, and he and Sanders laughed loudly.

Truman waited. Their laughter faded off. "Keep me informed."

───────

A little after three in the afternoon, Claber called again. "My 'research assistant' just contacted me. Someone called the hotline."

Truman moved around the pool table, discarding his solitary game, and leaned over the bar. He tossed aside empty to-go containers until he came across a notepad and pen. "What did they say?"

"It was a woman named Rachel. She said Natalie brought the girls to her house. Grey and Sanders are in route."

"Excellent." Truman swung away from the bar, pen in hand. "Give me her number."

Claber passed along the information.

"As soon as they reach her house, let me know. Where are you now?"

"Sitting at the post office."

Truman's phone dinged, and he pulled it back to check the call waiting. "Have to go. Call center's on the other line." He clicked over. "Yes?"

"Truman, I just got a call on one of the lines you tapped." Nigel's voice was barely audible over the sounds of telemarketers and customer support answering and making calls in the background. In between being a call center supervisor, he also worked for Truman, monitoring and collecting calls from any tapped numbers. "I emailed an mp3 to you."

Things were looking up. "Keep monitoring and tell me if anyone else calls."

"Will do."

Truman hung up and opened his email. Sure enough, he had a new message with an attachment. He opened it, letting it play over the speaker. The hurried conversation pratted off in French, and Truman had to play it twice to make sure he understood. But he got it. Natalie, the girl who rescued the kidnapped girls, used a phone to call her own cell phone, which was in her boyfriend Chris's possession. She wanted him to meet her at a local diner and take the girls somewhere safe.

Truman dialed Sanders' number.

"Yes—" Sanders began, but Truman interrupted.

"Belay your current destination. Go to Louie's Diner. The girls will be there."

"Yes, sir. We'll get them, sir."

"You better." Truman hung up and tapped his fingers on the counter top, feeling impatient and helpless. Who else was searching? The Bennett brothers. He called them.

"Yello," Danny Bennett said, his customary answer.

"Danny. You and Derek get over to Louie's Diner and provide back-up for Sanders and Grey. They'll be bringing the girls in."

Danny passed the information on to Derek, who yelled, "You got it, boss! We're on our way."

So eager. They all were. Now nothing to do but wait. Truman paced the hardwood floor, resisting the urge to call Sanders for an update. The phone rang, and Truman snatched it up. "Grey? Do you have them?"

"No." Truman heard yelling in the background, and Grey continued, "They drove away. We're chasing them. But I've got a visual. They're driving a dark-gray SUV with brown wood paneling. It's old and slow." Grey swore, then shouted, "Sanders! Watch the traffic!"

"I'll call the police," Truman said, his adrenaline kicking in. "We'll get a patrol to pull them over."

"Slow down, slow down, slow down!" Grey yelled. "Boss, we just lost them over a railroad track."

"Street names," Truman snapped.

Grey spat out the intersection names, and Truman called Officer Fayande. "I need you to get your men on this right away. Pull them over for reckless driving, expired tags, any excuse. Get them to me."

Fayande hesitated. "I cannot do this personally. I will alert the unit closest to them."

For a moment Truman's vision blacked, and red lights flashed in front of his eyes. "I need all your units! Get everyone on them!"

Fayande lowered his voice, the French accent thick in his whisper. "It will blow your cover. I'll be questioned."

Truman hung up. He couldn't handle Fayande's excuses right now, but in the back of his mind he also knew the man was right. He called Claber back. "Claber. What's going on?"

"I'm not sure," Claber said, sounding a bit rattled. "I'm still at the post office. Sanders said you sent them to a diner. The Bennetts said the same thing. I haven't heard anything since then."

"They're chasing the girls," Truman snapped. His mind whirled, trying to find an assignment for Claber. He had the big van and three men with him. Not exactly equipped for car chases. "Stand by for action. I'll call you with an assignment."

Sanders' number showed on the phone, and Truman clicked over. "What's the news, man?"

"We lost them."

CHAPTER 15

Sanders' voice was heavy with disappointment. "We're still surveying the area, but I don't know where they went."

Truman squeezed his eyes shut and pounded his fist into the pool table. He couldn't give in to the desperation wrapping itself around his chest. "Keep searching. I'll check back." He slammed the phone down on the green fabric, then grabbed a pool stick and snapped it in half.

The next call came from Fayande. "My patrol spotted them and gave chase. But they switched vehicles, and we haven't had any sightings since then."

"Fine." Truman felt no anger or disappointment, only a calm resoluteness. "I have no more need of your services."

"But—" Fayande started to respond, but Truman hung up. Instead, he called Claber.

"News?" Claber asked.

"No. We've lost their trail. But let's think here. Where would they go?"

"To America," Claber said instantly.

"Exactly." Truman smiled. "I want you to research the most likely route by road and through the woods. Chances are they won't use a legal point of entry because they've seen the police with me and they don't want to get caught."

"Makes sense. Then what?"

"Get everyone together. The Bennett brothers, Grey and Sanders.

Send two groups into the woods. I want you and two others back in the States, prowling the border."

Someone in the background let out an exclamation.

"What?" Truman barked. "Someone have a comment?"

"Just Hastings," Claber said, his voice less confident.

"What's his problem?"

"Apparently he has some concerns about the plan."

"Out with it," Truman demanded.

"He thinks it's a waste of time."

So Hastings had decided there were no boundaries, that he could insult and rage to his heart's content. Respect was still lacking.

"He doesn't have to go, then," Truman said, his voice icy calm. "Dispose of him."

"Sir?" Claber asked, and there was no mistaking his surprise.

"You had no problem doing it to McAllister's men. I'm tired of having my decisions questioned," Truman growled. "What hurts one of us hurts us all. Hastings doesn't want to help, fine. We don't need a broken wheel. Get rid of him."

Claber's voice murmured as a muffled conversation occurred in the van. Then Claber said, "He changed his mind. He's more than willing to help."

That's more like it. "Perfect. I want him in a rental car, stateside. He reports directly to you. I want constant surveillance on the likely points of entry."

"Yes, sir," Claber said, his voice hesitant.

What was the problem now? "This isn't difficult," Truman snapped. "Four people in the woods. Four in the States. You just have to research the likely entry points."

"But there could be dozens—"

"Then choose the best ones!"

"Yes, sir."

Truman took a deep breath, letting his rational self take over. "Get on this. I want detailed maps by tonight. Send Hastings and the Bennett brothers into the States right away. But you come back with the four going into the woods. We'll need to prep them with supplies for the journey."

"Yes, sir."

Truman hung up. He stumbled over to the bar and grabbed the whiskey. It looked like he still needed his contact with the police force. Truman pressed the preassigned number.

"Fayande," the man answered.

"I need you to arrest some people."

"On what charges?"

"Well, that's up to you, isn't it?" Truman consulted the notepad he'd used when speaking with Claber. "Let's start with Chris Coton and his girlfriend, Natalie."

————

Claber and the four men he'd selected to track the girls in the forest entered Truman's office. Their faces glistened with sweat, and he could practically smell their fear. It had come at a heavy cost, but Truman admitted to liking the respect the men had for him. He glanced at Claber. Claber's mouth twitched, a vein on his neck pulsing. He clutched a manila folder at his side.

Truman tapped his fingers on the wooden desk in a solemn staccato, letting the silence draw out. The men shifted about and kept their eyes on the floor.

"Well?" he finally said. "What happened? How did you and the police both manage to lose the girls?"

Sanders cleared his throat, straightening a little. He glanced at Claber, who gave a slight nod. "The last call Claber got on his hotline was at a gas station in Victoriaville. The caller correctly identified the car and the driver. We found the vehicle on the side of the road. It was empty. Either they proceeded on foot or they got a different car."

Truman kept his face impassive. "What are your projections? Where are they now?"

Sanders' Adam's apple bobbed as he swallowed. "Fayande has patrols watching the routes to the American consulate, the RCMP, and the border. They're looking for any vehicle with a blond driver and three or more girls in the car."

Already Truman saw the ways they could slip through. Dye the blond's hair. Get a different driver. Divide the girls. Head different directions.

He shook his head. The girls wouldn't think to do those things. "Let's assume they won't go to the authorities. We've frightened them into hiding. If the patrols don't find them, then what?"

Sanders looked to Claber for support. Claber shifted his weight just enough to increase his height by an inch before speaking up. "The girls could hide out at their rescuer's house."

Natalie's house. "We'll find them, then. And soon. Fayande will be arresting all parties involved in the rescue. I can't risk them contacting the FBI or American police."

Claber nodded. "I don't think they'll stay here, anyway. Hiding is a short-term solution. The girls want to get home. There's plenty of unguarded land between here and the New York/Vermont border. I've used that information to chart routes through the forest, assuming they'll avoid roads or public places. In case we don't catch them before they cross over, I've narrowed the points of entry down to seven. Vermont is most likely. Keep in mind, though, this only works if they slip across illegally. If they use the legal border stations, we'll lose them."

"But?" Truman prompted.

Claber's lips curled upward. "But they probably won't, for two reasons. Number one, we've scared them, as you mentioned. They know they won't be safe until they get to America. Number two, they don't have any legal documents. They'll think without proof, no one will believe them."

Truman nodded. "Agreed." Truman settled back and steepled his fingers. "Pack your gear and get into the forest. Keep satellite phones and anything necessary to sedate them until back up arrives." He swiveled his head in Claber's direction. "We've already got men patrolling the border?"

Claber nodded. "The men will circle around the city by car, and foot if necessary. I have four points of entry being watched. But there are several others I'd like to monitor, as well. I'd like a few more men to help."

Truman didn't have an endless supply at his disposal. All of the men not assigned to Claber were out on raids. "How many would you like?"

"Another four, if you can spare them. Just to be sure."

"How confident are you that the girls will use one of these points of entry?"

"Almost one-hundred percent." Claber opened the manila folder he held at his side. "Here are the maps I printed out with the different trails marked. You can check them yourself. While the border is several miles long, after we take out the legal routes, there are only half a dozen or so ways to get safely across the terrain."

Truman waved him away. "Good. As long as you have something substantial and not just guess work. I'll call in one of the raids and get you two more men. But that's all I can spare you. Notify all of our American agents. We need them on this, fast. If the girls make it to America, they'll find allies at every turn. We have to make sure we find them before someone else does."

"On it." Claber left the folder on Truman's desk and strode from the room.

Why couldn't all his men be so amenable? "The rest of you, you have your plan of action. Get your camping gear together and get into that forest. Any more questions?"

Nobody said a word.

"Go on, then. And I expect hourly updates!" Sara's face danced in his head, and he sat back hard as the men left the room.

Truman had one more item to take care of. At some point, the girls would call home. They might want help, or to simply tell their parents that they were okay. All he needed was one thirty-second phone call, and he'd have their location.

First, though, he had to tap their landlines. Rodriguez was already in Idaho, confirming Gregorio Rivero's identity. He could do that as well.

CHAPTER 16

Truman finished adding up all the jewels in the coffer, a nervous sweat breaking out across his forehead. He had almost three million here, if he could get to a buyer. He hardly dared leave the confines of his house, though. What if he were intercepted? Followed? McAllister might not recognize Truman's men, but if he had spies anywhere else, he'd find Truman.

He leaned back and chewed on his lower lip. None of that mattered, of course, if McAllister already knew where he was and was just biding his time to spring a trap.

Truman opened the desk drawer and flipped through a notepad. He only had one raid scheduled for this week, thanks to most of his men lallygagging around the border, looking for the missing girls.

The thought made Truman snarl, a flash of red anger blinding him. One week. One week with no sign. He wasn't ready to admit defeat, but he couldn't have his men parading around doing nothing for much longer. The girls hadn't gone to the authorities, they hadn't tried to call home, and they hadn't appeared at the border. Which left only a handful of options: either they were still in Canada somewhere, they were dead, or they were still making the journey.

His phone rang, and he glanced at Claber's name before answering. "Tell me you've got good news."

"Depends on what's good news," Claber said, a note of confidence in his voice. "Did Hastings call you?"

"No." Truman frowned. "Why?"

Claber hesitated just a moment, then said, "He found the girls."

Truman jumped to his feet. Hastings. He'd been surveying an entry point in Vermont. "Where is he now?"

"That's a very good question," Claber said. "Apparently Everett made his way out of the forest yesterday. He and Hastings met up. Then today they ran into the girls as they crossed the border into a city park."

Truman nodded. "So we know they're in America." He paused. When Claber didn't continue, he prodded him, "But that doesn't tell me where Hastings is."

"I don't know. He wasn't able to apprehend them. They created a scene and ran off. He told me he was going to hunt them down before they could go to the police."

The information overwhelmed Truman, and he sank back behind the desk. "He found them. Then he lost them. And now he's hunting them. Do we have any agents at the local PD?"

"No. But Hastings told the girls the police are on our side. That should deter them."

Truman nodded. "Good. I'll call Hastings, find out if he has them."

"His phone's off. I can't reach him."

"Then I'll try Everett," he snapped, losing patience with Claber's constant need for direction. "In the meantime, get all the men to Vermont."

"On it. I've got Alfred with me. I'll get the Bennett brothers and Sanders over here too."

At noon the call center called. "They used a phone to call Idaho," Nigel said. "And I've got that address. I'm emailing it to you along with the message."

"Thank you," Truman said. "Let me know as soon as you get another." He opened the attachment and played the message. Truman listened while a teenage boy told Mrs. Rivera that the girls were going to Maryland.

Nothing more, but it was enough. Maryland. It gave him a definite trail to follow. He jabbed his finger at Claber's number.

"Yes?" Claber answered.

"The girls are going to Maryland," Truman said. "Realign your trajectories."

"I'm on it."

The girls couldn't hide now. The possibilities from Vermont to Maryland were minimal.

CHAPTER 17

The girls never appeared in Maryland. After days of waiting, Truman ordered the Bennett brothers into the Adirondack forest to search for them, since that was the only other way out of Vermont.

And then silence. Two days passed with no updates.

Truman spent the time organizing elaborate raids for Grey's team in Michigan. When Claber finally called, Truman couldn't understand him because of all the yelling in the background.

"What's wrong?" Truman demanded.

"Huge. This is huge," Claber said, practically shouting in the phone. "I've got Derek with me. He saw them."

So that's who was yelling in the background. "Put him on!"

"Hang on, boss," Claber said. "He's a bit hysterical. He wandered the forest for a day before he found a street, and then it took him hours to get to a town and find a pay phone to track me and Sanders down."

Something didn't make sense. "But the Bennetts have a phone and a car. Where's his car?"

"He left it in the forest. He was a bit... confused." Claber's voice lowered. "Danny's dead."

The shrieking in the background intensified. Surely Truman had heard that wrong. "What?"

"She killed him!" Now Derek's voice, high and irrational, screamed into the phone. Truman backed his head away from the speaker. "That bitch killed my brother!"

"Derek. Give me the phone back. Derek. Thank you." Claber's voice returned. "As you can hear, he's not quite himself."

"Is it true?" Truman couldn't wrap his mind around the idea. He pictured Danny, tall and stocky. "One of the girls killed him?"

"According to Derek. But Truman, it was just a few days ago. They can't be too far!"

"Can Derek get you there?"

"Well, he's not exactly coherent. He can't remember what direction he came from."

"Derek needs to rest," Truman instructed. "Get him medical care. I need him better so that he can remember exactly where the incident happened!"

"Yes, sir."

"Claber. How many girls? Were they all there?"

"All three. It was the *Carnicero*'s daughter that killed Danny."

The *Carnicero*'s daughter. Did it run in the family? "Have you found anything out about him?" As soon as his daughter was back in Truman's hands, he planned to offer her up for a huge ransom. More than enough to make up for all the trouble she was causing.

"Found a place of employment. Getting contact information a bit trickier, though. Apparently he has more than one name."

"Well, try and track that down." Truman bit the words out, doing his best to mask the anger he felt. "This is priority. Take Alfred off the surveillance team and put him on this full-time."

"Will do."

———

Grey had just finished reporting on their last raid when Rodriguez knocked on the study door and let himself in.

Truman looked up, annoyed. He needed Grey to hurry and finish so they could discuss next week's raid. But his report was taking hours, thanks to Truman's inability to focus. "It better be important."

"It is, sir," Rodriguez answered, bobbing his head. He held the phone out to Truman and waved it. "Nigel from the Alberta call center is on the line. Says he has to talk to you."

Nigel was one of the only people that had his actual phone number. And email address, for that matter. Truman opened his palm and beckoned with his fingers. Rodriguez placed the phone into his hand, and Truman pressed it to his ear. "Do you have something?"

"Yes," Nigel said. "I got a tap for you. Wasn't long enough for a location, but I'm emailing the recorded message."

"Excellent," Truman said, unable to resist the hope tightening his throat. "Keep me informed of anything else." He looked at Grey and Rodriguez. "Dismissed. Grey, I need to borrow your phone. Go over next week's raid with your team."

Grey left his phone on the desk. Truman glanced at it before opening Nigel's email. His heart pounded in his ears so loudly that he decided to read the transcription rather than listen to the recording. He read it twice and then jabbed his finger at Claber's number.

"Sir?" Claber answered.

"The girls called home. We have to act fast. I don't have their exact location, but I got the city they're in. And they said they're going to the police."

Claber caught on without Truman having to spell it out. "I'll intercept them. Where are they?"

"Remsen, New York." Truman tapped his fingers on the desk. Opening the top drawer, he pulled out his agent directory. "We have an agent in the PD at Sweden, Pennsylvania. Five hours away."

"Send me his number. I'll call him."

"No." Truman inhaled. "I will. Stand by. I'll call you with the plan." Hanging up with Claber, he picked up Grey's phone and dialed the Pennsylvania number.

"This is Captain Jefferson."

"Captain." Truman took a deep breath. Rarely did he have to contact this man. "It's Alexander King." He used the name on his American passport, the one his American contacts were familiar with.

A short pause, and then Jefferson continued, his voice smooth and calm. "Yes. How can I help you?"

Truman kept his words encrypted. "Did you hear about that kidnapping in Idaho?"

"Idaho?" Computer keys clicked in the background. "Oh, yes, the four girls. I heard about that when it happened. Why?"

"I've lost something."

"Can I help you find it?"

"If someone finds it, I need you to get it."

"Will I recognize it?"

"Yes, you'll know it. Just call me if you notice anything."

"Sure. Will do."

Truman hung up. He knew that, behind Jefferson's confident words, he was sweating and anxious. Truman paced the office, resisting the urge to call the police station closest to Remsen. He couldn't be the one to tip them off. It had to come from Jefferson.

His phone rang, an unknown number with a United States prefix. "Yes?" Truman answered.

"I'm a block away, using a pay phone. I think I've deciphered your message." Jefferson's usually friendly voice sounded jittery. The man was the typical police officer; fit, dark hair, mustache, a warmth in his smile that made people trust him. That was a valuable asset. "A fax came in from the Little Falls PD twenty minutes ago, telling us to watch for the three surviving girls and immediately call them if they show up. I just distributed it to all the officers. Do you have something to do with this, King?"

Truman knew from his tone that Jefferson hated him at that moment. Kidnappers, people who would hurt young girls, were the quintessential bad guys. Truman pulled on his lower lip. He didn't have time to explain the entire situation, yet somehow he had to keep Jefferson's allegiance. "It's not what you think. But yes, they are important to me. One of the girls—her father is a vigilante. We're using her to hunt him down."

"King, those girls—they need to go home."

Truman lowered his voice, putting a threatening element to it. "Jefferson, we chose you for a reason. How does your wife like that seven-thousand square foot house you bought five years ago? Does your son like his new Mustang? Weren't you planning on repeating that vacation to New Zealand next year? Or maybe you'd prefer that they think of you as the dirty cop? Do you really want them to know where that extra inheritance came from?"

Silence reigned, and Truman knew he had him. Jefferson, like most people, couldn't bear the personal consequences that would come to his family. "All right. What do you want me to do?"

"I need you to send a fax to the police departments around Remsen, New York. Put an official signature on there saying this is the most up-to-date information. The girls are in danger. Top secret case. Anyone who sees them must swear to protect them and not give away their presence." Nothing like appealing to a policeman's protective nature. "They need to be brought straight to you before anyone can see them. Then get yourself to an isolated location so you can receive them. Let me know when they're on the way."

Truman paused, thinking through his next command. He wanted to follow this through in person. Could he risk it? Yes. This was big enough. "Get me the address. I'll meet you there." Which meant he had to catch a flight to New York, right now.

"King, if I sign this, it's going to come back to point to me."

"Tell everyone this is so top secret they must destroy the fax after reading it. Tell them there can be no evidence that the girls were ever there."

"They won't buy it." Jefferson's voice was flat. "It's too suspicious."

"Not coming from you," Truman soothed. "They don't suspect you. They'll believe you if you say your orders come from the FBI or Homeland Security or something. Make it believable, Jefferson."

"Got it." Jefferson's mellow voice was even and formal again. "I'll call you as soon as I know anything."

"I'm sure you will." Truman disconnected, unable to keep the smile off his face. A line from one of Shakespeare's lesser-known plays, *Cymbeline, King of Britain*, paraded through his mind.

That opportunity,
Which then they had to take from 's, to resume
We have again.

Dialing Claber's number, he headed back to his room and started throwing things into a suitcase. He shifted through a shoebox of passports and tossed the American one in as well. He nudged Barley and rubbed the dogs belly.

"I'll see you soon boy. Keep everyone safe here." He gave him another pat and straightened, all business.

"Game plan," he said when Claber answered. "I'm flying to New York."

"Before you come, you should know," Claber said, an ominous note in his voice.

"What?" Truman braced himself.

"We backtracked into the forest and found the Bennett brothers' car. We also found Danny. Boss—she bludgeoned him to death."

"How?" Truman demanded. "How could she do that with Derek right there?"

"He wasn't with Danny. By the time he got there, it was too late."

"But he did see the girls?"

"Yeah. But they have two boys with them. They're picking up

allies, P

CHAPTER 18

Truman stood on the paved circle drive, reviewing the raid briefly with Grey to make sure he and his team felt prepared and competent. Grey and team climbed into the black cargo van and headed down the mountain.

Truman waited until they were gone before making his own exit. He paused next to his yellow Camaro. Better take a car that wasn't so flashy. He backed one of the old black cars out of the garage. It clunked all the way down the gravel drive, and Truman hoped fervently it wouldn't die on the way to the highway.

Claber called just as Truman reached the bottom. "Jefferson says the girls are in custody in Rome, New York. The police are following orders to the T, and Jefferson expects to have them before nightfall."

Truman gnawed on his lip. "I won't get there in time. I'm on my way to the airport now. Can you meet him?"

"I'm on the eastern side of the state. I'll head that way, but the girls will beat me."

Jefferson would hate this. "Have him hold them somewhere for a few hours. One of us will be there shortly."

"I'll call him."

———

An hour and a half later, Truman checked into the Quebec International airport terminal as Alex King. His phone rang while Truman handed his matching credit card over to the attendant. He missed the call, but before he could grab it to check the caller, it began ringing again.

Thanking the attendant and securing his passport and tickets, Truman backed into a corner and answered. "Hello."

"Boss." Claber's voice hissed through the receiver. "The brats got away again."

What Claber was saying was absolutely impossible, and it took Truman several seconds to find his voice. "That can't be."

"It is. Remember those two boys? They followed the police cruiser and caused an accident. They've all vanished."

Truman couldn't breathe. Here he was with a plane ticket in hand, ready to have the girls in his possession. And once again, they had evaded him. "Find them," he said, and his voice shook. "Find them, or it's your head!"

He shoved his phone into his pocket and stared at the boarding pass. He didn't need to go right now, not if the girls had vanished again. McAllister's timeline was about up, and he still needed to finish planning his escape route.

He stepped back in line at the terminal. He had no power here, and he hoped they wouldn't have a problem changing his departure date by four days.

———

Alone again in the big house, Truman double-checked his luggage, making sure he had the essentials. Then he went through the jewels in the safe, counting and adding. All accounted for. And he'd make several million off them, as soon as he found a buyer.

He ignored the crushing anxiety that built in his head. These things took time. A trinket in this city, another in a different city. Selling the jewelery couldn't be rushed, not if he wanted to get the best price.

There was always Ebay.

The thought drew up the corners of his mouth, but just as quickly, he sighed. Too easy to track.

The early morning hours crept on, and Truman spent the majority of them tracking western routes in Alaska and comparing them with the ability to fly out to several different island groupings. His escape had to be remote, invisible, and perfect. His lids began to close around two a.m. He stretched out on the couch and fell asleep.

He didn't wake until noon when Barley licked him right across his nose. Bright midday sunlight streamed through the windows on the second floor. Barley sat back in the middle of his stacks of papers.

"Thanks, boy," he said with only a hint of sarcasm as he gathered maps and google printouts from under Barley's large paws. Truman blinked at the bright sunlight that was flooding the corner of the room where the couch sat nestled against a wall. He glanced at his phone, surprised no one had tried to contact him.

He wandered into the kitchen and poured himself a bowl of cereal. He tried Jefferson first. After a few rings, a mechanical voice said, "The mailbox is full. Please try again later."

Not a good sign. Pausing before he poured the milk, Truman called Claber. "Any news from our contact?"

"No. I did hear from Alfred; he believes he found a flight itinerary for Gregorio Rivera. It has contact information we don't have. Could be fake, but it's something to explore."

"Yeah, do that. He'll make a mistake soon. His daughter's life is at risk. Were the girls found?"

"I haven't heard anything."

"I'll try Jefferson's office number." An idea popped into Truman's head. "Claber, put Sanders in charge. I need you here."

"There?" Claber sounded a little ticked off. "But the girls are here."

"You're the only one who's ever accompanied me to sell the goods. You're the only one I trust. I need to set up a plan with you to sell these jewels. They do me no good sitting in a safe in the closet. Leave the van with Sanders and get up here."

Appealing to Claber's vanity worked. "I'll drive up in the Bennett brothers' car," he said. "I'll be there in a few days."

"Hurry. I'm flying out in three."

Truman hesitated before calling Jefferson's business line. For some reason, the man wasn't answering his phone. Truman hoped he wouldn't have to remind him about his loyalties.

———

Truman scanned the online newspaper one more time.

A car pulled into the garage. His phone buzzed on the table. But none of these things pulled him away from the headline on his tablet.

"Pennsylvania Cop Kills Himself."

The front door opened, but still Truman didn't stir.

"I'm here," Claber said, entering the room. "Didn't you see my text?"

"I ignored it," Truman answered, reading the article again. "Jefferson's dead."

"Who killed him?"

"He did." No other policemen were thus far indicated in the coup. Several unknowingly aided him, assuming his orders came from his superiors. "They raided his office," Truman said. "Confiscated his computer."

Claber gave a low whistle. "Will it point back to us?"

"No. The man was too smart for that. He wouldn't leave anything that would incriminate him." But a trickle of worry crept down Truman's spine. Jefferson might have left a trace somewhere. A notepad. A phone number. Something. He shrugged it off. "At any rate, he's dead now. Worse, the FBI probably have the girls."

Neither of them spoke for a few moments, and then Claber said, "So that's it, then. We're through? The little sluts win?"

Truman shook his head. "We can't quit, man. We can't! We have too much at stake. The girls are our only option. We carry on. Pack a bag and load up the car. Tomorrow we'll head out, you to sell those jewels and me for the States. Tonight we rest."

"There's one other thing," Claber said. "I left Derek Bennett with Sanders, but he's a mess. I don't think he'll be much help to the mission."

Truman felt bad that they'd lost Danny. He tried not to think about the Rivera girl, though he couldn't help regarding her with a mixture of fascination and curiosity. "I'll call him tomorrow and bring him home for a bit. Let him relax."

———

The sound of heavy vehicles driving across the gravel woke Truman. He lay face down on his king-sized bed, the blue sheet damp under his mouth. He stumbled out of bed and peered out the sliding glass door. Bright morning sunshine danced across the wooden slats of the balcony, and he squinted, trying to see who was arriving at this time of day. Grey and his team weren't expected back until tomorrow.

He jerked back from the window so quickly that he stubbed his toe on the end table. Wincing and swearing, he found his pants and yanked them on.

"Claber!" he yelled, throwing the door of his room open and running into the hallway. "Claber!"

Another door opened and his second-in-command stumbled out, wearing only boxers and the beginnings of a beard. "What is it, Boss?" he grunted.

"McAllister."

That was all he needed to say. Claber was awake in an instant, running back in to grab a shirt and a gun. It appeared McAllister's patience had run out.

Truman ran a hand through his hair, mind blanking. It was only him and Claber here. The others were out on assignments. His suitcase and the jewels were in the car, ready for departure. He ran into his office and grabbed the file folders with all of his contacts' information.

There was a loud banging on the front door. Truman could hear it three stories up.

"Let's go!" Truman hollered at Claber. "To the garage!"

"Truman!" The voice roared as though from a speaker.

Barley began barking. Truman looked back but couldn't see the dog. He risked a glance out the nearest window and quickly ducked. Four black GMCs surrounded the front of the house, blocking the front door. Several men had machine guns trained at the building. Truman looked at his pistol. A lot of help this would be.

"Time's up, Truman! We're coming in!"

Truman streaked past Claber, his face flushed. "Go go go. Down. Barley! Come! Get everything out of the car and into a van. Our only choice is to push past their blockade. Barley!"

They ran down the stairs, Claber stopping to grab various valuable art pieces. Truman ignored them all. Suddenly he hated this house, hated his father, hated this life of subterfuge and deception. Grinding his jaws together, he hurtled into the garage, Barley barking behind him. The metal door of the garage began to ping as the men outside opened fire. Truman popped the trunk to the car, and together they hauled their suitcases out and threw them into the van. Claber jumped into the driver's seat and Truman sank into the passenger seat. He looked out the door, but Barley wasn't in sight. "Barley!"

"We can't wait," Claber snapped, the van engine sputtering to life.

"Barley!" No sign of him. Why hadn't he followed Truman into the garage?

"Close the door!" Claber ordered. "I'm opening the garage!"

"Not yet—" Truman started, but Claber had already hit the control. Truman swore, slamming the door and sliding low into the seat.

Bullets began pinging against the bumper before the door was halfway up. Claber hit the gas. The top of the van screeched as it skimmed under the door. Claber drove in a crazy motion, avoiding vehicles and knocking over men. A bullet shattered the windshield, and Truman threw his arms up instinctively. Then they were jolting down the gravel hill.

"Don't look back," Truman grunted. "Just get them off our tail. Head for the airport." *Sorry, Barley.*He felt guilty for putting so much value on an animal's life, but he hoped the dog could save himself.

In the back of the van he had about four million dollars worth of jewels. It wouldn't pay off the ten million on his head. "We need those girls. We've got to find them before I have no chance of paying off my debt."

Claber didn't respond.

A million for the necklace, a million for the redhead, and maybe two million for the *Carnicero*'s daughter. Someone with a vendetta against the *Carnicero* might even pay more for her. On the other hand, the *Carnicero* could afford a hefty ransom. Either way, with eight million and the money from his accounts, he might be able to buy back his freedom. Might.

CHAPTER 19

"Excellent work, Alfred." Truman paced around the dim motel room in Sleazeville, California, restless with nervous energy. Alfred's sleuthing into the *Carnicero* was paying off. Now they had contact info to go with the name. Truman pressed the phone closer to his ear. "Even if the email we have for the *Carnicero* doesn't work, I'm sure his employers have a way of contacting him.

"Not only that," Alfred said, "but if they know we've tracked them down, they'll pressure him to accept our offer."

Either that, or they'll make silencing us a priority. The grim thought crept into Truman's mind uninvited. He made a conscious effort to loosen his jaw, rubbing at the sore muscle by his ear. "Right. I have another assignment for you."

"Yes?"

"Go back to Idaho. I want surveillance on the girls' houses. If you see police coming or going, make note. Check their mail every day, even if you have to sneak into the mail truck to get it before they do. Anything from the girls or the FBI, grab it."

"Yes, sir. I'll head that way now. I should get there tonight, if I hurry. But just me, for all four houses?"

Truman considered the question. "I know it seems like a lot, but you won't have anything else to do. This will keep you vigilant. I'll send Sanders out to join you."

"I'll let you know what we find out."

Truman hung up the phone and called Claber. "What time's your meeting with the dealer?"

"In about two hours."

Truman could practically hear the sunshine of Panama pouring through the phone. At least Claber had safely made it to South America. With any luck, McAllister had no idea where they were now. "Call me as soon as the deal's done."

"Right."

Sanders was next. Truman thumbed through his contacts and pressed the name. "Sanders, it's Truman. I need you to assist Alfred in Idaho. Call him and meet up with him."

"Sir?" Sanders said. "I'm with Derek. Bennett," he added, as if Truman didn't know. "Do you want him to come with me?"

Translation: the man wasn't ready to handle anything on his own.

"No," Truman said. This might work out really well, after all. "Tell him to stay in New York. Lay low in a motel. I'll be heading east soon."

"Got it. I'll get in touch with Alfred."

Truman put the phone down and rubbed his forefinger and thumb together. California was the other side of the continent from Victoriaville; also from where he wanted to be. He hoped it would throw McAllister even further off his trail. If his contacts were extensive, and Truman suspected they were, he probably had people monitoring the arrivals at airports on the east coast.

Truman risked a quick glance through the blinds, checking out the dingy street below. Vacant. He drew back, hoping no one had spotted him. How good was McAllister? Did he have Truman's American alias? If so, it wouldn't take him long to hunt down Alex King.

The dismal thoughts were easier to entertain than the optimist ones. He tried to picture finding the girls, selling two of them for ridiculous amounts of money, and keeping Sara with him. He couldn't keep her safe unless she was with him. There were bad men out there, monsters. Criminals.

He wasn't one of them. He supported more than a dozen men and families. He worked hard to make sure he wasn't hurting anyone personally. Sara had to see that.

By lunchtime the next day, Truman felt like an imprisoned man. He couldn't stay here much longer.

His phone rang. Alfred. He turned the speaker on and leaned over his phone. "Yes?"

"I got a letter here from one of the girls."

Truman could hardly believe it. He'd known it was only a matter of time before something broke through, but he'd started to feel like he'd been locked up forever. "Read it to me."

Alfred read the brief letter. Truman knew even before Alfred reached the end that the letter was from Sara. He could tell from the way she wrote.

The letter gave nothing away. Sara mentioned only that they had been found by the FBI and they were safe. "What do you think?" he asked Alfred.

"Well... she doesn't say much. Do you think it will lead us to her?"

"Best to have all our bases covered. What's the postmark on the letter?"

"Four days ago."

"What city?"

"Cleveland, Ohio."

Truman pulled up another website. "That's good enough for now. Let me know of any other developments." He studied the locations of FBI offices in Ohio. They had field offices in Cincinnati and Cleveland. But the girls wouldn't be at offices. They would be sequestered away in a private location, unknown to the rest of the world.

What he needed was an inside man.

He got on the phone again, grateful at least for this piece of useful technology. He had spoken to Grey briefly after McAllister's attack on the house, telling him to get to a different state than the one they'd just raided and wait for his call. Now, at least, he knew where he wanted to send that team. "Grey, I want you, Rodriguez, and Everett to go to Ohio. I need an employee roster for all the FBI agents there. You'll probably have to get one of our police officers on the job."

"I don't have a list," Grey said. "Do we have anyone in Ohio?"

Truman sat on the motel bed and startling rifling through his papers. What used to be organized files in a cabinet was now a mess of papers tossed about on the unused second bed. At least he'd managed to grab this stuff before fleeing the house. "Yes. Adam Dunn. I'll text you his number. Be careful with him; he's an informant only. Don't push him too far or he'll back out."

"Won't the police know where the girls are?"

"No." Truman shook his head. "They won't even know the girls are found, if the FBI are keeping it quiet. Just tell him you need a roster with all the FBI agents in all the offices, big and small, across the state. I'll start narrowing it down from there."

"Okay."

Invigorated, Truman hung up the phone and began packing. Game plan. Finally. He'd start in Cleveland, where Sara had mailed the letter. At least he knew she'd been there. Time to catch a flight.

He made a call to the front desk. "Taxi, please. To the airport. Charge the card on file. I'll sign when I get down."

Truman walked again to the tinted window of the hotel room. He peered through the blinds, staring out at the flat, brown landscape. A few planted trees dotted a park across from the motel. Children piled out of a red Hyundai, heading for the playground. He picked up his cell phone and dialed Sid.

"Hello?"

The sleaze practically oozed through the phone. Truman

suppressed a grimace. "Sid. I want to continue our negotiations."

He could imagine Sid sitting up, raising one black eyebrow. "Oh? Are we still on? It's been weeks since I've heard from you."

Truman gritted his teeth. "I'm re-acquiring the girls as we speak."

"Fantastic," Sid purred. "Where can I meet you? I have a very wealthy client with an insatiable appetite."

A blue Firebird pulled up behind the red Hyundai. Nice car. "I'm flying to Ohio. Prep your passport. I'll call you when I get there."

"Do you have passports for the girls?"

Truman paused. He had not, of course, thought of this. He'd never dealt in this business before. "No."

"Text their pictures to me and I'll take care of it. Make sure you change their appearances before you take the pictures."

Where was Sid planning on taking them? Out of the U.S., naturally. But then, where?

Truman pushed the thoughts from his mind. Didn't matter. Once he sold the girls to Sid, they were no longer Truman's concern. It was Sid's responsibility to get them out of the country unnoticed.

He'd probably go through Mexico. The authorities were pretty lax on those leaving the States. "I'll get it done." He hung up the phone, not wanting to hear any more comments from Sid. He couldn't shake the repulsive feeling that clung to his skin after speaking with Sid. Made him want to take a shower.

He didn't want this life. He never had. As soon as he got Sara back, he was retiring. Somewhere quiet, remote, and warm.

CHAPTER 20

The phone rang between the two beds. Truman leaned across the pillow and answered it, wiping sleep from his eyes. "Yes?"

"Your taxi's waiting."

"Thank you."

Truman stood and tucked several files back into his suitcase. Something flashed in the street below, and Truman leaned his forehead closer to the window, narrowing his eyes. A glint of metal on the driver's side window in the Firebird. A reflection of the door frame?

He recognized the sniper gun a split second before the wall next to his head exploded. He threw himself facedown on the floor seconds before another bullet punctured the window and buried itself in the hotel door.

His heart thudded in his chest, and he frisked his hands down his body. No sign of injury. Somehow, he had to get out of here and into the taxi without being shot. He lifted to his elbows and pulled himself away from the window. "Probably a man in the hallway," he breathed to himself. His mind felt sharp and alert, adrenaline enhancing the details of the room. He yanked his phone out of his pocket and called 911. Getting the police out here wasn't good for him, but it might scare McAllister off as well.

He could punch through the plaster wall to the next room. And then what? Just keep punching through walls until he got outside?

He gave the information to the dispatcher and snapped his phone shut. More bullets pinged around his room and he flinched, smashing his face into the ground. He couldn't reach the motel phone, but surely they heard the noise. Not that they were likely to send any heroic person up to save him.

He reached a hand up onto the bed and felt the folder that had held the documents. Information was more valuable than lives, and he couldn't lose all this. His fingers closed around the folder and what was left of its contents. It only held half a dozen sheets. He cursed at them and lifted his hand to get more of the documents. Another bullet pierced the window and flew over the bed. Papers flew everywhere and he ducked as he was showered in glass and a small barrage of office supplies. His fist closed over a handful of papers, and he shoved them up his shirt.

Truman slipped his pistol from his pants and slithered to the door. There couldn't have been more than four people smashed into that Firebird. At least one was down there shooting. Which meant there were, at most, three inside the motel, waiting to take him out. Taking a risk, he stood and pressed his eye to the peephole.

A man stood outside the door, leveling a gun at the card swipe.

Truman swore and jumped out of the way just as the bullet blew a hole in the door. Not wasting a moment, Truman stuck his gun through the newly formed opening and fired. A cry and a thump let him know he'd hit his target. Swinging the door wide open, he hurried from his room, stepping over the body.

Stairs or elevator? Stairs were bad for getting trapped. Elevator was bad if McAllister's men were in there. Truman hit the elevator button and leveled his gun at it. He kept his body angled so he could survey the hallway, eyes sweeping the corridor.

The elevator opened, revealing a security officer. This was the motel's offering? One man, and probably unarmed? Truman let out a sigh and lowered his weapon. Good thing he planned for himself.

"There." He pointed to the fallen gunman. "He tried to kill me."

The security guard's eyes took in Truman's weapon. "Give me that gun."

Truman wanted to argue the point, but didn't really have time. He slapped the weapon into the man's hand, hoping his bank account had enough for him to buy another.

"Don't go anywhere," the guard commanded, and hurried to the dead man.

Whatever, Truman thought. He stepped into the elevator and pushed for the lobby. The door slid shut. "Plan, Truman," he whispered. "What's the plan?"

Get out. That was the only plan. McAllister still had two or three men running around the motel, trying to find him. He straightened his meager pile of pages into the folder, hoping to look business like.

The elevator came to a halt, and Truman flinched. Someone had to be waiting here.

Then he heard the sirens and breathed again. McAllister wouldn't risk a gun fight with police outside. He hoped the taxi hadn't left.

Then again, he didn't know how long McAllister had been trailing him. He might know everything.

No, he couldn't know about Cincinnati. That had been decided only minutes ago.

Anxious patrons filled the lobby, being comforted and consoled by the motel staff. Outside, the police were busy setting up a perimeter around the hotel, and Truman realized a taxi wouldn't be able to get in. He stepped around the distressed guests and searched the buildings across the street. A man stood outside a yellow cab in front of Pizza Hut, shielding his eyes with one hand and looked toward the motel.

That had to be his taxi. The police probably made him move.

The front doors were guarded, keeping anyone from going in or out. Truman slipped around the corner to the side exit. No one stood by it. Taking a deep breath, he pushed the door open and stepped outside.

His foot barely graced the sidewalk before someone grabbed his arms and shoved his face against the brick building. He tensed as hands slid down his body, frisking him. And then he was spun around.

"What are you doing?" a police officer barked. "Everyone is to remain inside."

Truman's heart pounded frantically. How would he get out of this? He scanned the officers, looking for a familiar face. He'd been here a year ago with one of his agents, and he'd met several officers under the guise of a foreign doctor.

Behind the man who detained him, Truman spotted an officer he'd met. Hopefully he remembered him. Truman waved his arms. "Sergeant Chrisler!"

The policeman looked over and focused on Truman. "Yes?"

Truman jogged toward him, keeping his facial expression stiff. "You probably don't remember me. Officer Kim introduced us, just over a year ago. I'm Dr. King?"

"Oh, yes." The sergeant nodded vaguely, and Truman doubted he actually remembered. But using Kim's name earned his trust. "Are there any injured inside? How fortunate that you were here."

Not really. "I haven't heard of anyone yet. But I received a call on my pager, and I'm needed at the hospital." He pointed across the street. "I have a taxi waiting for me. Can I go?

"Of course." With a wave of his hand, he dismissed Truman.

Too easy. Truman hurried over to the taxi.

"Are you Alex King?" The driver looked him over.

"Yes." For a panicked moment Truman thought he'd left everything in the motel room; a quick pat-down assured him that he still had his passport and wallet, along with the cell phone. Everything else, all his files, his luggage, his other weapons—he gritted his teeth. He could only hope the maid cleaned out his room and tossed the info, or every agent he had would soon be receiving an unwelcome visit.

And since it was a crime scene, chances were good that the police would get to it before she did.

For a brief moment he entertained the idea of rushing back inside to grab his files. It wasn't worth his life, though.

"So glad you made it out," the cab driver said.

With an effort, Truman forced a smile. "Crazy. I had to leave all my stuff behind." He climbed into the cab, his body stiff. Truman considered again what he'd left in the room. *It doesn't matter*, he told himself. He was retiring. The whole network could dissolve.

Still, he would have to warn his agents about what was coming.

He thumbed through his phone, making sure he still had all his contacts.

"What's going on?" the driver asked, gesturing at the police cars and arriving ambulance as they drove away.

"No idea. Airport, please." How on earth had McAllister tracked him to California?

Had McAllister somehow figured out his American name?

My ears are stopped, and cannot hear good news, So much of bad already hath possessed them.

The Two Gentleman of Verona had so much depth for a comedy. Truman clenched his jaw and dug his fingernails into his hands. He couldn't catch a plane here. "If you can skip the international airport and take me to a regional one, I'll just charter a jet. Here." Truman handed him a wad of cash. "This should cover any extra expense."

The man glanced at the money and his eyes widened. "Right away."

Truman settled back and closed his eyes, fighting a migraine. That was all the cash he had left.

———

"Here's what I've got." Grey glanced up over the sheet of names in front of him, meeting Truman's eyes across the table. "These are all the agents employed in Ohio."

Truman took the sheet of paper and scanned the names. None of them meant anything, and only six had more than a name and phone number. He was just glad to be alive and out of California. McAllister wouldn't be able to trace him here. Derek had procured a motel room in Cleveland using his name, which would be unknown to McAllister. "What are these highlighted names?"

"These are the agents who have been reassigned in the past week. All of them are in Cincinnati."

Truman nodded. "Then whatever's going on isn't here in Cleveland. We're in the wrong city. How did you get this information?" It would take weeks of stake outs for him to know which agent had been reassigned.

"From the FBI database. This was all I could get, though. The security encryption for any other information was too high. I have no idea where these agents are going or what they'll be doing. I only know they were taken from their current assignments to different ones."

Derek Bennett leaned over as well. Truman couldn't think of him without thinking of his dead brother, Danny. Derek's eyes had a muted desperate wildness to them, but the rest of his expression was serious and professional. Truman had his concerns about Derek's mental stability, but he kept them to himself.

Derek cleared his throat. "So we need to get to Cincinnati and find the girls. Can Grey get into the computer system again?"

At least he sounded sane.

Grey shook his head. "All I could get into was the employee roster. I can't access anything else. You'd need a much better hacker than me."

"This is enough to start. You did good. Looks like we're going to Cincinnati." Truman ran his finger down the names, mouthing them to himself. "Rodriguez."

The short Hispanic man pulled himself away from the wall. The veins on his overworked biceps stood out under his white tank top. "Boss?"

"You and Grey get all the information on these names as you can. I'm looking for someone we can threaten. There has to be more at stake than their own lives, or they won't care. Someone with a child, a family."

Grey nodded. "Yes, sir."

"Let's go, then. Derek, you're with me. Rodriguez and Grey, you're in the other car." It was time to switch rental cars, anyway. He had to keep things new all the time.

Cincinnati was a four-hour drive from Cleveland. By the time they got there, Grey had worked his networking magic over the phone. He explained what he'd found as they hunched over the small table in a Motel 6.

"Most of these agents are single, but I found several with families. Some have teenage kids, which we could kidnap and hold as collateral..."

Truman zoned out for a moment. More kidnappings? The nervous sense of panic he'd felt the day McAllister attacked fluttered in his throat again. This wasn't what he wanted. *I'm retiring*, he reminded himself. *I have to do this so I can get out.*

"I especially paid attention to the female agents. They're usually easier to intimidate. Here are a few possibilities." He circled the names "Crystal Florence,""Abigail Belsun," and "Sonja Andreasen" with his blue pen.

"Crystal's single," Grey continued. "No immediate support group, and she has a little girl. Abigail is also single, has a preteen son, and lives in an apartment building in the center of town. Sonja is married, but her husband is currently out of the country. If we tell her we have agents on him as well, she'll do anything to protect her two beautiful babies."

"Babies!" Derek yelled "I am not taking care of babies."

Grey rolled his eyes. "Toddlers, children, whatever. They're three and four."

Truman narrowed his eyes and considered the women. A smile crept to his lips. "Good work, Grey. We'll keep an eye on all three, but Crystal is our focus."

Grey nodded and took a long sip from his giant cup of soda. "She was an easy one to track down from the start. Her answering machine says, 'You've reached Crystal and Rachel! Leave a message!'" He imitated the high-pitched tones of a woman.

"Rachel could be a sister," Rodriguez pointed out. "Or a roommate."

Grey's lip curled up in contempt. "Only if said roommate squeals like a two-year-old."

"Easy way to find out," Truman said. "You have the address?" Anxiety bubbled in his chest but he kept his voice calm. He reached toward the floor to pet Barley and paused mid air. He kept forgetting that the dog was gone. Rerouting the movement, Truman brushed at a non-existent piece of lint on his pants.

"Yep. Good ole' phone book."

Another reason why Truman had no land line. Or cable, or internet, or anything that could be traced back to his house.

A lot of good it had done him in the end, of course. "Grey, you're with me. Rodriguez and—" he hesitated before saying "Bennett." It felt so strange to include only one man in that name. "Derek. Start staking out Cincinnati. Look for side streets that aren't on the map."

"Big city, boss," Rodriguez grunted.

"Then we better get going," Derek said, his nose wrinkling. "Lots a ground to cover."

Truman ignored them. "Let's go, Grey."

CHAPTER 21

Rodriguez was right about one thing: Cincinnati was huge. Florence lived twenty minutes away from the motel. They pulled into the three-story apartment building a little after four p.m.

"Think she's home?" Grey asked.

"What is her job position?" Truman counted doors until he saw the one he assumed was hers. The shades were drawn tight. Looked pretty quiet.

"Employee roster said guidance counselor. I didn't get any more than that. All I know is that another case was added to her load."

"What makes you think it has anything to do with the girls?"

"Nothing, besides the fact that she lives here and could access them easily. Why relocate someone when you've got locals?"

Made sense. "Well, let's hope the new case is a group of emotionally distraught teenagers." Truman's gut twisted with an irritating stab of guilt. He forced it away. He couldn't think about what he was about to do to this woman's life. "She probably works normal hours. Let's let ourselves in nice and quiet."

Rentals, especially apartments, usually didn't come equipped with security systems or special locks, which worked in their favor. In less than five minutes, Grey had the place open. Truman pulled on his black gloves before touching the door.

Even without the lights on, evidence of children was everywhere. An umbrella stroller propped itself up in one corner. Shoes and dolls littered the couches and carpet. Sippy cups decorated the kitchen counters and floor.

"This is all from one child?" Truman asked.

"That's what it sounded like."

They continued down the hallway, stopping at a pink bedroom with see-through curtains around the pint-sized bed. "Stay in here," Truman instructed. "I'll try and find something about her cases."

As cluttered as the house was, Florence's office was pristine and organized. Truman broke open the lock to the file cabinet and rummaged through various thick green files. All of the patients were assigned a number next to their name.

Five names threw him for a moment until he remembered the boys who had helped the girls escape the police. So they were in custody now, too. Interesting. He'd have to investigate them further.

She'd already met briefly with each teen and written down a few key points of interest. Truman scanned the reports and then pulled out Sara's file. His breath caught in his throat, and he reread the words three times before they sank in.

"Dealing with unwanted pregnancy resulting from sexual assault."

No. It couldn't be. His hands trembled, the paper shaking in his grip. Finding the chair, Truman sank into it. She was pregnant.

How? How could she be pregnant? His mind spun back to the nights in the mansion. He'd tried so hard to keep her safe, to keep her out of Sid's hands so this wouldn't happen to her. Not Sara. He dropped the papers from his hands and sank into the nearby chair, burying his head in his hands.

Sara was his. Who would have the balls to do this to her? Had McAllister somehow found out? It was impossible.

Truman raised his head as his second-in-command entered his mind. Claber. Stupid, stupid idiot he was. Claber had been bucking Truman's control for years now, and Truman had placed her right into his hands. He'd asked Claber to watch over them, to escort her to and from his room.

Truman jerked to his feet and punched the wall. The lancing pain that flew up his hand and wrist did nothing to alleviate his fury. There was no forgiveness for this. Claber would pay. He ran his hand down his face, trying to calm himself.

He'd worry about this later. Truman closed the cabinet and returned to the princess room. His hands shook. "She's it. I found all the paperwork."

Grey leaned forward, excitement flashing in his eyes. "Did you get an address to the safe house?"

Truman shook his head. "The FBI are far too careful for that. No address, not even names. But it's definitely them." He made no mention of Sara's pregnancy. "You have equipment in the SUV?" Per Truman's commands, Grey had traded in the black van for a dark SUV.

"Yeah."

"Tap all the landlines to the complex and bring up tape and rope. Then make yourself comfortable. We'll hide out here until they get home."

CHAPTER 22

A little after six p.m., Truman heard the sound of a key turning in the front door. It banged open, followed by the smell of fast food and the sound of little feet running down the hall.

"Hey Rachel!" a woman's voice called. "Don't you dump your bag on the ground! Come and get it!"

"I want to check on Mr. Hugs."

The cheery toddler voice brought an image to Truman's mind of a dimpled girl with golden ringlets and red ribbons. From his spot crouched behind the open bedroom door, he spotted a fluffy teddy bear wearing a dress and propped up on the pillow of the bed. Mr. Hugs might be having a gender crisis.

"Put your bag away first. Go give him a hug and come back to eat. You don't want your chicken nuggets to get cold!"

"Okay."

The footsteps resumed their hasty patter toward the bedroom, and Truman tensed. He pushed down the sense of unease, the bitterness over being forced to take this role.

She bounded into the room, only as tall as his thighs, straight brown hair in pigtails. *Don't frighten her,* Truman cautioned himself. He waved at Grey to stay back.

Rachel picked up the badly dressed bear on the bed and squeezed it tight. Truman stepped up to the bed and crouched next to Rachel, careful not to alarm her.

She looked at him, her eyes widening.

"Rachel," he murmured, "call your mother. I need to talk to her. But don't tell her I'm here."

"Is it a surprise?" Rachel whispered, mirroring his tone.

Truman nodded in relief. A surprise, of course. He pointed behind the door. "I'll hide over here so she won't see me, okay? For the surprise." He smiled again and the little girl grinned back.

"Mommy, come here!" Rachel chirped, her voice unsuspecting.

"Rachel, it's time to eat."

"It's really important, Mommy. Someone wants to see you?"

Truman slipped back behind the door, his muscles tightening. But Florence didn't react. "I've already met Mr. Hugs. Your food's getting cold."

"Not Mr. Hugs. Someone else. Please, Mommy?" She glanced at Truman, and he nodded, giving her a smile.

Florence sighed, and then her footsteps came down the hall. "Rachel, really." She stepped into the room. "We can play later."

Truman closed the door behind her and prepared himself for a physical attack. "We'd rather talk now."

Florence whirled around, and her mouth dropped open. Before she could utter a sound, Grey stood behind her, pressing a hand against her lips. "Shh," he murmured. "No need for that."

Truman moved to the bed, sitting next to Rachel and stroking Mr. Hugs. "We're not here to hurt you." He picked Rachel up and held her in his lap. "We just want to make a deal. Right, Rachel?" He smiled at her, and she looked toward her mother.

"Mommy?"

"Here are the conditions," Truman said, meeting Florence's clear blue eyes. Her chest heaved with repressed anger, features tight. "In a few moments, my comrade is going to move his hand. If you scream or try to leave the room, we'll be gone. And we'll take someone along with us." He stroked Rachel's pigtails. "Agreed?"

She nodded. Grey moved his hand. Florence grabbed it and twisted it around, her smooth blond hair escaping her bun. Grey gasped out as she pinned him to the ground.

Truman pulled out his gun and held it behind Rachel's tiny head. "Crystal," he said softly, "I wouldn't do that."

She lifted her head, spotted the weapon trained on her little girl. His heart pounded, desperate that she not call his bluff. He didn't have it in him to shoot this child. He couldn't.

But Florence didn't know that. In that moment, Truman saw all her resolve, all her FBI training melt away. "What do you want?" she whispered.

"Sit down."

She let go of Grey and settled onto the floor, her tight black skirt sliding up her thighs. Grey stood up, wincing and rubbing his body.

"Since you insist on not being civil, we won't be either. Rope, Grey."

Grey began fishing around in his cargo pants while Truman tucked his gun away and turned to Rachel. "We're going to play a game with your mom. We're going to tie her up while we talk to her. Do you want to play?"

Rachel nodded and held out her hands. Truman pushed them down gently. "No, we don't need to tie you up." He looked back at Crystal. "You know where the girls are?"

"You're The Hand," she breathed, understanding dawning on her porcelain face. She tugged against the rope on her wrist.

He scowled and leaned forward. He was becoming too well-known in legal channels, thanks to those girls. He did not want to be recognized on the street. "All I want are the girls. That's it. Get them to me, and I'll leave you alone."

She gave a laugh. "They're safe in FBI custody. I couldn't get them for you if I wanted to. What, you think I can waltz you into the safe house?"

"Just give me the address."

"There is none. Even if you had it, you wouldn't be able to break in. It's impossible."

The woman was far from broken. By tomorrow, she would tell the FBI all about Truman and his plans, and the girls would be whisked away somewhere safer, unknown.

Unless he had collateral.

"You'll find a way. Until then." He stood up, lifting Rachel with him. "Rachel's going on a sleepover."

Florence fought against her bindings. "You can't. You won't get away with this."

"I will." He arched an eyebrow. "I always do. And this one is too little to run from me."

"No!" Tears formed in her brilliant eyes. "Don't take her!"

"Mommy?" Rachel began.

Truman handed Rachel to Grey. "Take her and Mr. Hugs to the car. Don't forget her chicken nuggets."

Grey nodded, accepting the child and leaving the room.

"No!" Florence started to scream, but Truman cut her off, knocking her to the floor and kneeling on her chest. She gasped, and he released some of the pressure. Sara's pregnant figure still pressed at the back of his head and made focusing difficult. Claber would pay.

Truman covered her mouth with his hand and took a deep breath. "Listen. I won't hurt your little girl. I promise you. But if you don't do exactly as I tell you, you will never see her again. That is also a promise."

Florence shook under his hand, tears rolling down her face. "I'll do it," she whispered when he moved his hand. "I'll do whatever you want."

Truman nodded. "And no tricks. We're watching and listening." He moved off her body slowly as her eyes darted around the room. She thought he'd bugged it. No, but he'd tapped the phone, and that would have to be good enough. "Where's your cell phone?"

"In the kitchen," she whispered. "But I don't know how to get you the girls."

"We'll work on that."

"Please don't hurt her." She sniffed, no longer an FBI agent, but a vulnerable mother.

"I won't. And I reward those who help me. The two of you will rendezvous when the deal's over. Then I'll send you both far from here. Anywhere you want to go. It will be like a very long vacation." His eyes hardened, piercing hers. "But if you go to the police with this, if you try to stab me in the back, only Rachel will go. Understood?"

She nodded. Truman knew she hadn't given up. She would work every angle she could, try to catch him and save everyone. But in the end, her love for her daughter would win out. He reached behind her and loosened the knot. "Should take you about twenty minutes to work that free. What you do after that is up to you. But we'll know." With that, he turned around and walked out.

All the way to the front door, he prepared to run, waiting for her scream. It never happened.

———

"Transaction went through. Money deposited."

Truman read through the email, glad that Claber hadn't called. Even after three days, Truman didn't think he could mask his fury via a telephone call.

Somewhere in South Dakota, Grey had just given Rachel to Alfred. He would care for her and Mr. Hugs until Florence pulled through. Truman was paying him to be the perfect babysitter: Wendy's every day, walks in the park, the zoo, whatever she wanted.

He no longer cared about his accounts. He just wanted to get out of debt unscathed and have enough to live a simple life somewhere, with Sara and her child, the child that he would raise as his own.

Everyone else in the hotel room was asleep. The only light in the room came from the glow of his tablet. Truman typed out a quick response to Claber. "I don't need you there anymore. Book a flight to Cincinnati as soon as you can. Let me know your info when you have it."

He sent the email and rubbed his jaw, trying to release some of the tension. Claber would pay for what he'd done.

His phone vibrated in his jeans, and Truman scowled. Better not be Claber. He pulled it out, surprised to see the "Restricted" label. "Hello?" he answered.

"The girls are being transferred tomorrow." Florence's voice shook over the line, and Truman knew she hated this even more than he did.

"Transferred?" Truman straightened and switched on the dim light by the bed. Derek moaned and rolled over on the other bed, and Rodriguez twitched on the floor.

"Yes, transferred," Florence confirmed. "The twin boys were transferred to New York today. Tomorrow it's the girls' turn.

The digital clock on the nightstand showed just after midnight. "And you just found out about this?"

"You're lucky I found out at all." Florence inhaled. "They could've been transferred under our noses and none of us would know where they went." Accusation laced her words. Like this was his fault.

"Good thing they told you, then. Do you have a plan?"

"Yes. The agent that called me was concerned for their mental well-being, said they aren't responding well to being moved. He asked me to come in and do one last session. I suggested something even better. I volunteered to drive them to the rendezvous."

The plan clicked into place. "And you deliver them to me instead."

Truman's heart rate sped up. No one suspected Florence. She was the good girl, just like Captain Jefferson, just like himself, until McAllister. He'd been the good guy.

"Yes," she whispered.

"Where's the rendezvous?"

"I can't say," she said, and he knew she guarded as many FBI secrets as she could. "You'll have to meet me here in town."

"Got it. Take them to a fast food joint. Leave them in the car but go inside to order. One of my men will take them and the car while you're inside. Send me the address and the time to expect you. And you know what will happen if we see signs of anyone else." She wouldn't risk the cops. Who would they look for? Truman certainly wasn't going to be there.

"What about Rachel? How is she?"

"She's good. She's not here, but she's good."

"How can I trust you?" Her voice cracked and she choked back a sob. "I swear I'll kill you if you've hurt her."

"You'll see her again soon. I'll leave a rental car for you at the fast food restaurant. There will be a new passport for you and information inside. Go to the airport I indicate and catch your flight out of here. Rachel will be waiting for you."

"You're—" she took a deep breath. "You're an evil man."

He paused. He couldn't blame her for thinking that. "I'm doing the best I can. It's business, after all. I have to get those girls back."

"Some of us do business that helps other people."

"Not you," he returned, then felt bad for throwing her betrayal in her face. He didn't need her second guessing herself now, not when they were so close to the finish line. "We all do what we need to watch out for ourselves and the people we love."

She didn't respond. He pushed back his misgivings. If she backed out now, she lost her daughter. She wouldn't. She couldn't.

"All right," she whispered. "I'll have them for you tomorrow."

The phone went silent.

No time to worry about her. Truman lay back in bed and dialed Sid. "I'll have the girls tomorrow. When can you be here?" The sooner he enacted this deal, the sooner he could wash his hands of it.

"I'm in the middle of a business deal in Thailand," Sid said, loud music and voices echoing in the background. "I'll be here for five more days. As soon as I'm free, I'll head your way. Try not to lose them, Truman!" Sid laughed, a booming, irritating sound. "I might have to start charging a processing fee!"

So funny. Truman hung up. He thumbed though his contacts until he found McAllister's number. He stared at the name, dread weighing heavy on his chest. He tried to remind himself that McAllister couldn't trace the call, at least not if it were quick. He planned out a two-sentence conversation and hit "call."

The phone rang seven times before Truman hung up. Not even a voice mail. Truman knew better than to hope that meant McAllister had dropped off the planet.

By 5 a.m., the men were driving around Cincinnati, scoping out the city with new eyes. Grey had returned from South Dakota about two hours earlier, and though exhausted, he sat in the back of the SUV drowning himself with Red Bulls. Today was too important to sleep through. Derek sat beside him, tense and wild-eyed.

Rodriguez would wait at the chosen fast food place, McDonald's, for Florence. When she went in to place the order, he'd take her car.

"These are the girls," Truman had said, showing him their photos over and over again. Rodriguez had to make sure Florence delivered the right people. "Number one." Truman stared at Sara's open face, the cheerful hazel eyes and perpetual smile. "Number two." Rivera's daughter, with her dark eyes and dark hair that were so reminiscent of the *Carnicero*. "And number three." Murphy, the stunning redhead that should fetch a decent price. "Make sure you have these three."

"Take them to the warehouse?" Rodriguez pocketed the photos.

"No. Corner C." They'd scoped out several possible places to meet up with the girls. Truman needed a secluded area with plenty of visibility, just in case Rodriguez was being followed. Corner C was under an overpass. A trailer park flanked it, surrounded by broken down cars, run down buildings, and tall grasses. No one would notice his vehicle sitting out front, and no one would pay attention to the exchange of prisoners. Only when he knew they'd evaded the police would he take the girls to the warehouse. It hadn't been hard to find an abandoned one in this old city.

That was last night. Hopefully Rodriguez would remember his part today.

Truman took a deep breath, enjoying the smell of the car, of being out of the motel room. Rodriguez couldn't mess this one up.

In less than six hours, the girls would be in his possession again.

His phone dinged, indicating an email. Truman pulled it out. It was from Claber. Truman memorized the flight date and time. In two days at six p.m. He'd go alone. None of his men needed to know.

———

"I've got them."

Rodriguez's heavily accented English carried through the phone, and Truman allowed himself a rare smile of satisfaction. "Meet me at the rendezvous in ten minutes." Closing his cell phone, he looked at Grey and Derek. "He's got them. We'll wait under the overpass."

Grey hooted in triumph and Derek nodded. "Time for them to get theirs," he whispered. The mad look in his blue eyes had lessened, revealing a somber, smoldering expression. Truman didn't want to think about the emotions broiling underneath the mask.

Truman tried to maintain a calm exterior, to not show how much this meant to him. He dialed Alfred. "You have Rachel?"

"Yes," Alfred said, his tone mildly perturbed. "She's wearing me out. When do I stop playing grandpa?"

"Soon. Get across the border and head to the airport. I'll text you the destination and flight. Wait there for Florence, then make sure she and Rachel get on that flight."

The radar on the dash emitted several high pitched squeals, and Truman shot a glare at Derek. Derek slowed down. Wouldn't do to get pulled over now. None of the police in the area worked for him, and he couldn't take the chance of being delayed—or worse, recognized. At least one FBI agent in the area knew his description.

The phone beeped in Truman's ear, indicating another call. "Gotta go."

Derek parked under the overpass and the car idled. Truman glanced at the caller ID. Rodriguez. A pit formed in his stomach, and he shoved it away. It was just an update. "What?"

Rodriguez's voice carried over the tiny speaker, his words punctuated with hisses. "Two and Three in vehicle. One escaped. Meeting at Corner C."

Truman clenched his jaw and dug his fingers into the palm of his hands, the pit in his stomach forming into a hard rock. "Got it." He threw the phone and swore. Such a simple thing. Hop in the car, hijack the girls. And the idiot let one get away.

"What happened?" Grey asked, leaning forward from the back.

Truman took several deep breaths. Two and Three in vehicle. One gone. Sara was number one. "One of the girls got away."

"Shall I pursue?" Derek growled. "Hunt her down?"

Truman struggled for a moment. She didn't love him, but maybe he could still earn her love.

But she might never forgive him for what Claber had done. That bastard. He'd ruined everything.

"No," he said softly. "Let her go." *Sara. That's all I can do for you.* "We'll wait here for the other two."

CHAPTER 23

Truman didn't have much time to reflect before Rodriguez pulled up in Florence's FBI car.

"Quick," Truman ordered, jerking his head at Derek. The Bennett boy was easily the biggest of them all. He didn't expect the girls to go without a fight, and according to Derek, the Rivera girl had killed before. "Help Rodriguez get them in."

Derek jumped out of the car. Truman looked over his shoulder at Grey. "Grey, they'll sit by you. Keep their heads down."

Rodriguez guided the two teens, one with long dark hair and the other with a perfect, slender body and wavy red hair. Both struggled in his grip, twisting their shoulders and trying to pull away. Truman stared at them a long moment. It had only been a few weeks, but it seemed he hadn't seen them in forever.

Derek grabbed a hold of the brunette and locked eyes with Rodriguez. Rodriguez shook his head, and tug-of-war ensued microseconds before Derek released her and grabbed the redhead.

Grey opened the doors, and Rodriguez smacked his captive in the head. "Get in!"

Rivera's eyes darted to Grey, then to Truman. He saw her expression crumple. She knew, then. They were defeated. Truman turned back to the road, scanning for police or any followers. He took no pleasure in their recapture. He just wanted out.

All the doors slammed shut, and Derek climbed into the driver's seat. He raised an eyebrow at Truman, and Truman nodded. The road was clear. Straight to the warehouse. He looked back at Rivera and Murphy. "Heads down."

They complied, though with Grey on one side and Rodriguez on the other, they didn't have a lot of options.

Truman faced forward again, a sick feeling ruining his earlier good mood. He wanted to hit the dash, scream, curl up and cry. He'd lost Sara, or rather, he'd never had her. Instead, he had these two girls who just wanted to go home to the families who loved and cared for them.

I've crossed the line, he thought. *I've gone too far. And there's no turning back now.*

His father would be proud.

———

Rodriguez delivered the girls to their designated closet inside the abandoned warehouse. Truman's head pounded. They drove the rest of the way to the motel in silence.

"Listen," he said when Derek parked the SUV. "I know we have to lay down the law. But do not hurt those girls. If they have any damage, any marks on their skin, their value goes down. And absolutely," he paused to glare at each man, hoping to make them feel the weight of his ire, "do not molest them.

"Here's the plan. Each morning, we deliver food to the girls and take them to the bathroom. Sid will be here in a few days. We just have to keep them hidden that long. Rodriguez, you have tomorrow."

He nodded.

Truman got out, slamming the door behind him. The men followed him into the motel room, but he stopped them before they got comfortable. "Grey, you've been traveling all night. Stay and rest. Derek, take the SUV. I want you by the warehouse at all hours. If there's any sort of activity there, get the girls out. Drop Rodriguez off in town."

"In town?" Rodriguez said, furrowing his brow. "You need some shopping done?"

Shopping. It was the furthest thing from Truman's mind. "No. Find out where the cops hang out. Keep your eyes and ears open. I want news." And maybe a small part of him hoped to find Sara. But just a small part. "Find a sleazy bar somewhere in town. Buy off the tender with a couple hundred, tell him we need some new looks for a couple of girls. But don't pay him. Be back here around seven." Truman needed to get some cash before he could actually pay anyone.

The men headed out, and Grey crashed on the other bed. Truman stayed awake in the dimly lit room. He called Sid and told him he had the girls. Just as promised, Sid would be there in four days. And he was bringing cash.

Truman's headache persisted. He gave in to the urge to drink and took a swallow of whiskey. The alcohol burned all the way up to his ears, but did nothing for his headache.

He locked all the bolts and again tried to ignore the restless despair that flooded his bones. The angry words from *The Rape of Lucrece* exploded behind his eyes.

Thou foul abettor, thou notorious bawd;
Thou plantest scandal and displacest laud.
Thou ravisher, thou traitor, thou false thief,
Thy honey turns to gall, thy joy to grief.

"I found one," Rodriquez reported two days later. "Corner of Fifth and Vine. Decently priced, too. They're ready for your makeovers. Just show up."

It was the perfect opening for Truman's exit. Claber's flight arrived in two hours, and he'd been wondering how to get out alone. He stood, pulling on his baseball cap. "I want to see it. Make sure they won't blow our cover."

"They won't," Rodriguez began, but Truman raised a hand. His